HOLIDAYS IN OCEAN ALLEY

ELAINE L. ORR

Other Books by Elaine L. Orr

Jolie Gentil Cozy Mystery Series
Appraisal for Murder
Rekindling Motives
When the Carny Comes to Town
Any Port in a Storm
Trouble on the Doorstep
Behind the Walls
Vague Images
Ground to a Halt
Holidays in Ocean Alley
The Unexpected Resolution
The Twain Does Meet (novella)
Underground in Ocean Alley
Jolie and Scoobie High School Misadventures (prequel)

River's Edge Cozy Mystery Series
Newsprint to Footprints
Demise of a Devious Neighbor
Demise of a Devious Suspect

Logland Mystery Series
Tip a Hat to Murder
Final Cycle
Final Operation

Family History Mystery Series
Least Trodden Ground
The Unscheduled Murder Trip

Lifelong Dreams Publishing
www.elaineorr.com

All rights reserved.
LCCN: 2015917772
ISBN-13: 978-1518607943

DEDICATION

First to my family, always.

.

ACKNOWLEDGMENTS

I have spent a great deal of time with family members who were in care facilities, including assisted living. What I know comes largely from watching staff provide excellent care, even under trying conditions. More power to them.

CHAPTER ONE

Scoobie in Charge

HAVING A MILD stroke does not have to be a big deal. Unless you're standing on a step ladder three weeks before Christmas, hanging garland. When you break a wrist and ankle at the same time, it's hard to run a bed and breakfast at the Jersey shore.

Aunt Madge has had to ask her Harry to run the B&B. That means my Jolie will manage the real estate appraisal business she and Harry usually run together.

What could possibly go wrong? If you knew my family, you could imagine possibilities.

For some reason, I was the one who was finally able to get Aunt Madge to agree to spend a few weeks in Ocean Alley's Silver Times assisted living apartments. Today, she and I were in the living/kitchen/dinette combo of her apartment.

"Please, Aunt Madge. Just wiggle your fingers one more time."

"Adam, if I could, I would wiggle a certain one at you."

"If you don't do one more wiggle, I'll write something rude on your cast when you're sleeping."

"You do that and I'll, I'll…"

"Kick me?" I grinned at her, and then lowered my voice. "You promised to call me Scoobie."

Aunt Madge shifted slightly in her wheel chair. "I said I'd try to remember to call you that silly name."

"Good enough." I glanced at the clock. It sits above the kitchen sink, which Aunt Madge says is no bigger than a Kleenex box. "Dinner starts at five. I'll wheel you to the dining room. I think you're having New England clam chowder and biscuits for supper."

"I want to go to the bathroom one more time. You can push my chair in and I can pivot and take care of my own business. Please."

I turned the wheelchair and we moved from her living area through the bedroom to the large bathroom. Jolie and I hide Madge's dogs in there when we sneak them in for a visit. It works until Mister Rogers smells food. Then we're outed.

After closing the door to the bedroom, I called Jolie. "Scoobie here. Reporting from detention central."

"Hey. Is she any better?"

I knew Jolie didn't mean Aunt Madge's bone health. It's the first time either of us had seen her really down. For the few days in the hospital she was her usual self, but when she assented to move into assisted living for four to six weeks, she seemed to wilt.

"She didn't say she wanted to skip supper, so that's good."

"Thanks so much, babe. I've never done three appraisal visits and two write-ups in one day."

"You know I don't mind. I think I'll sit with her for supper, and then head home."

"Harry said if we go to the B&B about six, he'll feed us."

"Are we talking his leftover muffins or real food?"

"He's ordering in Chinese. He practiced making sugar cookies, but they burned and he's airing out the downstairs."

Harry sometimes joins Aunt Madge for lunch. He was widowed for many years before he married Aunt Madge two years ago. Their combined ages are 161, with Aunt Madge having a nine-year edge. Harry says that since they married he has forgotten much of what he knew about cooking, so he's gotten good at ordering in. I think he's practicing selective retention.

Jolie and I said goodbye, and at the sound of a flush, I stuck my head in Aunt Madge's bedroom. "You transferred back to your chair yet?"

"You didn't hear a splat, did you?"

"Did you say splash or splat?"

"I'd be grateful if you'd push me down the hall."

I walked to the now partially opened bathroom door, leaned in, and grabbed the back handles of her chair. "If you can transfer so well, I'd say we should look for a scooter for you."

"One of those things the tourists speed down the boardwalk in? I'd be afraid I'd kill someone."

"At least you wouldn't be wearing a wet bathing suit. Where's your sense of adventure?"

Madge appeared to think about the scooter idea as I pushed her toward the dining room. "I suppose it would be worth a try. They're awfully expensive, though."

"Lester said he could get you a deal." Lester is a sometimes-pushy Ocean Alley real estate agent who is known for listing houses too high, and giving Jolie and Harry grief when the appraisal won't support an offer. He's also cheap.

Aunt Madge laughed loudly, and then covered her mouth for a second. "Lester and his deals."

"I'll call him tomorrow."

She put a hand over mine on the handle. "You're good to me, Scoobie."

"Flattery will get you everywhere." I touched her lightly on the top of her snowy head. Usually she changes hair color every few weeks. She uses some kind of temporary color that washes out. It occurred to me that her spirits would improve with one of her more vibrant shades of red.

When we got to the dining room, Lance Wilson waved to us from a table near the back of the room. He's in his mid-nineties, and is on the local food pantry donation committee with Jolie and me. Last month he sold his house in Ocean Alley and moved to Silver Times.

"Oh, good. Lance is back." Aunt Madge turned her head to look at me. "I'll sit with Lance. You go on home."

"Sure. I want to stop by Melvin Hamburg's place. He came in for an x-ray today but wouldn't stay to get treated."

We were nearing Lance as Aunt Madge asked, "Why ever not?"

"I can tell you that," Lance said. "Got his finger caught in his car door. His middle finger. Doesn't want to get it splinted."

Melvin lives in the independent apartments that adjoin Madge's assisted living building on the large campus, which also has a nursing home and town homes. He can take stubborn to a new level. Since he was an instructor when I got my radiology technologist degree, I figured I owed him at least the pretense of saying no one would think he's flipping the bird at people all day.

I left Madge and Lance to fill each other in on their recent hospital stays, Lance's being for a hernia acquired when he tried to move his big-screen TV himself, and walked to the independent living building. After buzzing Melvin's apartment twice I gave up, and went to look for Lester.

The air was crisp, and it was in the upper thirties, decent weather for December at the Jersey shore. Since it was after school let out for the day, I drove carefully down the narrow side streets. One of the silver bells that hung from lampposts had come partially unfastened and blew in the light breeze. I was about to pull out my mobile phone to call the public works office when a patrol car slowed to a stop under the swinging bell.

"Better them than me." I kept driving.

Ocean Alley is almost two miles long but only twelve blocks deep. Each street that is parallel to the ocean is named for a letter of the alphabet, but the alphabet starts with B. The Great Atlantic Hurricane removed the old boardwalk and most of A Street in 1944. It's the main reason Aunt Madge bought a B&B that was four blocks from the ocean.

I drove through Ocean Alley's downtown, such as it is. The area near the courthouse has a small grocery store, the post office, a couple of law offices, and a few restaurants. We were lucky that Ocean Alley was fully built before the condo craze hit. There are lots of hotels and beach rental cottages, but it still has the feel of a small town.

I pulled into Burger King to look for Lester. He meets prospective clients there, which reinforces anyone's perception of him as a bargain-basement kind of guy.

Sure enough, Lester, unlit cigar hanging from his lips, was at a back table. A pile of paperwork sat beneath a glass of iced tea.

"Hey ya, Scoob, get your butt over here."

Lester isn't usually so friendly, so I figured he wanted something.

"How's the old la…Madge holdin' up? You tell her I said hello?"

I sat across from him. "She's getting better, but she'll be in that wheelchair a good while. You still know where we can get an inexpensive scooter?"

Lester leaned across the table. The distinctive mole on his cheek was no more than eight inches from my nose. "I got it outta the garage at that dump on Conch I bought, you know, for investment. I just..."

"Didn't you tell Jolie and me that dump would be a good upgrade for us?"

He gestured with the cigar. "After I get it renovated. Anyhow, old man Koester's daughter sold it to me with anything she left in it. She thought the scooter was toast, but all it needed was a new battery."

"That'd be great. What can we pay you for it?"

Lester leaned back and squinted. "How about I just rent it to her? Say ten dollars a week."

"That doesn't sound like much. You sure?"

"It's Madge. Plus, she can be my test driver."

JOLIE AND I WEREN'T about to let Madge be Lester's guinea pig, so the next morning we borrowed our buddy George's truck and took the scooter to Madge's place ourselves.

Jolie was the test driver, and I winced as she jerked the scooter forward. "Whoa! Look out! The up lever is forward, remember?"

"More or less. I'll take it down the sidewalk one more time."

"Just remember we need less backing it into car bumpers."

Jolie sped by cars parked next to the sidewalk, giving me her four-fingered wave without looking back. Her Santa hat blew off and her shoulder-length brown hair flew behind her. It would be better if the scooter had a down shift button.

I walked a few steps and picked up her hat, glancing across the parking lot as I did. Melvin's Ford Taurus was in its space. When we got Madge comfortable with the scooter, I'd check on him before I went to work.

Jolie turned and came toward me. She's the best thing that ever happened to me. We lost touch after high school. I'm not glad I dropped out of college to feed my former pot habit, or that she was hurt by an embezzling husband. But if we hadn't been through those times, we wouldn't have both been single when she moved back to Ocean Alley to live in Madge's B&B for a while. Our lives are better all the time.

She pulled to a stop a few feet from me. "Okay, with the tinkering you and George did and my scrubbing, it's ready for Aunt Madge." Jolie looked at her watch. "I think we have just enough time to help her practice before I have to be at the courthouse to do research on the houses I looked at yesterday."

"Yeah, I've got the eleven o'clock start, but I'll get groceries before I head to the hospital."

With me driving and Jolie standing on the side, we rode into the facility's dining room to greet the breakfast crowd. The only thing missing was a clown with a squirt bottle.

Jolie and I circled the four-person table closest to the door and drove back to the hallway.

Aunt Madge looked mortified. "Oh good heavens you two. What a treat."

Lance laughed. "Madge, had I known I'd have brought a starter pistol."

"Ahem." Mrs. Grand, the morning dining room attendant, did not look pleased as she called from across the dining room. "Jolie, you'll have to let the physical therapist teach your aunt to get on and off that thing."

Jolie nodded. I turned the key before standing. "Yes, ma'am."

Aunt Madge doesn't mind chastising us, but she didn't look pleased to have Mrs. Grand do it. In a sort of frosty tone, she said, "I look forward to a professional tutor."

I winked at her, and she added, "I bet I'm fully trained by the time Harry comes over for lunch."

THE THIRD TIME I buzzed Melvin's apartment, I was irritated. He needed to get his finger in a splint, and I can be as ornery as he is. I leaned into the intercom and spoke slowly. "I know you're up there."

"The hell with you Scoobie, get your ass up here."

"Nice." Fortunately, Melvin didn't teach the sessions on interacting with challenging patients.

When Melvin opened his door I had a hard time not laughing. He had used a teaspoon for a splint and scotch tape to secure it to his finger. "You were worried about an actual splint calling attention to your finger?"

"Get in, get in."

I did, and Melvin closed the door quickly. He knocked a small Menorah off the table just inside the door. I stooped to pick it up and put it back, this time further from the edge.

The independent living apartments are not huge, but they're twice the size of Aunt Madge's unit, and have a full kitchen. Melvin's place was crowded with several styles of furniture, in various conditions.

It only took a few seconds to take in Melvin's untied bathrobe over stained pajamas and the spilled box of cereal on the dinette table. He was not operating well with one hand. "Once you get it properly set, it'll hurt less. You'll be able to at least use your thumb and forefinger better."

"Can you put coffee in the damn filter?"

"I'll do it, but when you've drunk it I'm taking you to Doctor Gardner."

He started toward the kitchen. "I don't want to go to him. Take me to Doctor Knight."

"The new woman? Sure, if you think she can work you in. I hear she's pretty strict about people needing appointments." I looked at the spilled coffee grounds on the counter and stooped to pick up a spoon from the floor. "You sit and I'll make the coffee. You want cereal poured?"

"I 'spose." Melvin sat in a dinette chair.

"Why not go to Doctor Gardner?"

"We had a disagreement."

"About what?"

"Who his wife could sleep with."

I paused from separating a coffee filter from the pack and looked at him. "You're kidding."

"Wish I was. She hardly spent a week with me and was back with him. She got a new Buick out of the deal."

Doctor Gardner is about forty-five, tall, and perpetually tanned. Melvin is five-six at most and a wizened fifty-eight. I figured Doctor Gardner enticed his wife back to save the embarrassment of coming in second to Melvin.

CHAPTER TWO

Aunt Madge on the Prowl

I'VE NEVER BEEN one to take afternoon naps, but after the morning's therapy session and lunch, I had needed one. That nap was one reason I couldn't sleep in the wee hours of Saturday morning.

The therapist had also wanted an afternoon session to see how well I transferred from the scooter to the recliner and back. That gave Harry a chance to see me in action, as he put it.

I could tell Jolie and Scoobie had been more enthusiastic about the scooter than he had. But my husband is flexible. When he saw I wasn't going to fall and break my other wrist, he kissed me on the cheek and went back to the B&B to walk Mister Rogers and Miss Piggy. He has become my retrievers' favorite person.

The clock next to my bed said twelve-thirty.

Most people get sleepy from pain medicine. I get hyper and they still want me to take a pill before bedtime. I've tried hiding it under my tongue to spit out later, but it tastes terrible.

I sat up and carefully swung my uninjured foot over the side of the bed. Then I balanced my casted arm with the other hand. This would be a perfect time to take my scooter into the hall to practice. There is only one attendant on at night, and she stays in the office unless someone has a scheduled medicine or one of us pushes our help button.

Tonight it was Gina. I like her. She sat on my bed and talked to me the first couple of nights I was here, when I was awake half the night.

I moved onto the scooter, careful to place my good foot on first and hold onto the handle bar with my good hand. Then I swung onto the seat. The automatic door let me into the hall and I turned right to drive toward the game room, which is really a game niche. Lance keeps threatening to teach me bridge. I tell him I'd rather jump off one.

I stopped outside the laundry room. Was that someone talking? After a few seconds of hearing nothing, I started driving again, this time toward the dining room. I would not go beyond it, or Gina could see me from her perch in the office. I'm entitled to be where I want, I just didn't feel like hearing someone else warn me to be careful.

The three-point turn I did was nearly perfect. One more swing down the hallway I lived in and I'd feel confident enough to take the scooter onto the sidewalk outside the building before lunch.

Near the laundry room, a sound made me stop again. It was definitely a person, and it sounded as if they were grunting. I looked up and down the hall. The only other person up now would be Gina. If she was hurt, it would do no good to press the help button around my neck.

I pulled the scooter close to the door, turned the handle, and began to nudge the door with the scooter. The front tire squelched on the metal plate on the bottom front of the door, and I paused.

A grunting sound came again, and then silence.

I increased the scooter speed so the door opened fully. The laundry room held only the industrial washer and drier, a folding table, and a bin on wheels that staff used to take sheets and towels from the apartments to the laundry.

The bin was the only place a person could be. My scooter still held the door open, and the bin was only a few inches away. I reached its edge and pulled it toward me.

A man was facing the wall, his knees pulled to his chin. He was so still I felt sure he was dead.

I gasped and let go of the bin, then pushed the scooter's handle lever down to back up. The incessant beeping almost made me fall off the seat. I let go of the lever, expecting to hear doors opening and people entering the hall.

Nothing happened. Half of the other residents wear hearing aids. Still, how could they sleep through such racket?

Two more beeps put me back in the hall. I sped to its end and did another three-point turn. I needed to find Gina.

The building has three hallways, with common rooms that connect them. I peered in the dining room. Empty. Same with the television room. Where could Gina be?

I went back to the lobby, with its plethora of Christmas and Hanukkah decorations, and paused near a manger scene. The main doors swished opened and Gina walked in.

"Mrs. Richards. Why are you up?"

"Thank God. There's a body. Follow me."

Gina set her pack of cigarettes on a table by the entry and pulled her phone out of her jacket pocket. "Who? Who is it?"

"I'm not sure. In the laundry bin."

She was behind me, but I could tell she stopped. I turned. "Come on."

Gina began to jog and passed me. She pushed open the laundry room door, walked part way in, and then came back out.

"Mrs. Richards. There's no body in there. You must have been dreaming."

NO ONE CHASTISED OR MADE fun of me, but when Sergeant Morehouse arrived at my apartment I thought he was restraining himself. He's used to Jolie giving him a hard time, not me.

"So, Madge, you say he was facing the wall?"

"Yes, with his knees drawn up to his chest."

"What was he wearing?"

I leaned my head against the recliner. "Grey sweat pants, and a dark blue shirt. It looked like knit fabric."

"Like a golf shirt?" he asked, fingering a button at the collar of his own rumpled green shirt.

"Yes. But I'm not sure I remember a collar. I didn't look at him too long."

Morehouse was on the loveseat and Sondra Hewlett, the assisted living director, sat in a dinette chair about ten feet to my right. Gina had called her, which added to the embarrassment I felt.

"Madge," she began, "did it look like another resident? Someone who…"

I shook my head. "I don't think it was anyone who comes to meals."

"You been here how long, Madge?" Morehouse asked, and yawned. He probably had a busy day coming up. Even though he's young, early forties, it's not easy to do any work on less than a good night's sleep, much less police work.

"Just a few days."

"Glad to see that stroke didn't seem to affect you." He glanced at a small pad he'd been using for notes. "Thing is, Mrs. Hewlett here said she had Gina do a bed check. Everyone's accounted for."

"So I hear. I know what I saw." And I figured his reference to my stroke was Morehouse's way of saying maybe my mind was playing tricks on me. I could have kicked him with my good foot.

Morehouse turned slightly so he could look at Sondra directly. "When can you get the security cameras checked?"

She hugged a sweater tighter. "I've called our firm. They downloaded a two-hour period, starting about an hour and a half before Madge entered the laundry room."

She didn't say before I saw the man.

Morehouse nodded. "Good, good. All the hallways? And doors?"

"Separate cameras pan each hall. Everything's

covered."

Morehouse looked back to me. "Let me be clear. I don't for a New York minute think you're lyin'. But is there any chance you were confused? Maybe medication…"

I shook my head firmly. "I know what I saw."

He stood. "And we will study what we get from the cameras. Since so few people were awake then, those are our best bet."

"Of course." I glanced out my window and back at him. "I'm sorry to have gotten you up."

"No problem. Mrs. Hewlett, can you walk out with me?" When she agreed, he looked at me again, this time with a small smile. "I don't think you're nuts, Madge."

"I appreciate that."

I stayed in the recliner for several minutes, simply thinking and looking out the window. At night, the small shrubs that lined a nearby walking path looked like black blobs. They were not a comforting sight.

I'd known Sergeant Morehouse for at least ten years. While he might think I was confused, he would never say so.

Mrs. Hewlett was a different matter. She was new to Ocean Alley, having transferred from a facility in Philadelphia. She also wasn't terribly popular. I'd overheard two staff talking about their dislike of her plans to rework staff schedules.

Maybe someone wanted her job. But kill for a promotion? It would be easier to simply apply for a position at a different apartment or nursing home.

At lunch today, no, yesterday by now, I'd heard that she was more strict about enforcing rules dealing with how able a person had to be to stay in assisted living. Rumor was that she wanted to transfer a couple of residents to the nursing home because they took too much staff time. I didn't want to give her grounds to transfer me based on mental health issues.

I was convinced that someone had been in that laundry bin. I wanted to ask Sergeant Morehouse to look for hair or other indications that something more than sheets had been in there at one time, but couldn't bring myself to do it. He would think I was paranoid.

By now it was two-thirty, but I wasn't tired. I glanced around the small apartment. The walker I was learning to use was by my recliner, but Gina had parked the scooter near the door to the hall. She said it was to make space for Sondra and the police, but my guess was it was so I wouldn't drive through the halls again tonight. This morning.

A light rap on my door announced Gina. "You've been up a long time. Do you need any pain medicine?"

"It keeps me awake."

"How about just some Tylenol?"

"Thanks. That would be great."

She came fully into the apartment and headed for the locked medicine safe in the closet near the tiny kitchen area. She didn't speak as she extracted the pills and logged the dose.

When she turned to get a cup of water, I asked, "Do you think I'm crazy?"

"No." She spoke firmly. "I don't know what you saw, or if your eyes played tricks on you, but you aren't crazy."

"It's also what I heard." I took the cup in one hand and pills in the other, and popped them in my mouth. The cool liquid felt refreshing.

She took the cup from me. "Maybe they'll see something on the cameras. You want me to wait while you get into bed?"

"Probably a good idea." I let her adjust my covers and plump the pillow, but refused her offer to help me swing into the bed. "Thanks a lot."

After a minute in the dark, staring at the ceiling, a thought came to me. The entry doors were locked at night. But people tended to think of their space as a cross between a nursing home room and a private apartment. Almost no one locked their door.

Whoever was in the bin didn't have to leave the building, just duck into an apartment. If they were lucky, they wouldn't be on a security camera and could sneak out when it was calmer. Gina had done a bed check, not a thorough search of each unit.

I got up and slowly made my way to the hallway door, my casted arm resting on a small platform attached to the walker.

It felt good to flip the dead bolt to lock.

LOW VOICES woke me a few hours later. As always, I expected to be in our bedroom in the B&B, to see Harry or hear Mr. Rogers snore. Within seconds I was oriented and realized that the voices were just outside my bedroom door. Someone with a key had let themselves in.

"Maybe it was the pain meds."

"That's what we thought, but she insists no."

The first voice was Jolie's, the second belonged to one of the day shift staff, Martha, I thought. Jolie's words stung. How could she not believe me?

I sat up part way, leaning on an elbow. "I'm awake in here."

The door swung opened, whooshing slightly on the carpet. "So you are," Jolie said. "Feeling better?"

"I never felt bad." I sat up fully. "Can you bring my scooter in so I can go down to breakfast?"

Martha spoke from the doorway. "Finished half-hour ago. I made you a plate of eggs and bacon. Put it in your little fridge. Jolie can heat it for you." She turned to leave, and spoke over her shoulder. "Mrs. Hanson needs me to find her hemorrhoid cream."

Jolie sat on the foot of my bed. She looks younger than her thirty-one years, but today her eyebrows were knitted in a frown of concern.

"Nice to have your illnesses broadcast," she said.

"She doesn't even have them. Her late husband did, so she likes to look at the tube on top of her TV."

Her brows relaxed and she smiled. "For the record, I know you heard something that made you go into the laundry."

I made a shooing gesture. "Please get my scooter. And it registers that you didn't say I saw something."

She stood and saluted, the way Scoobie does sometimes. "Roger. I'll wait while you use the bathroom and we can chat while you eat."

"Perfect. Heat it for me, would you?"

I took my time. It's the key to not falling. My

clothes for the day were already on a hanger on the towel rack. I put on the knit top festooned with snowflakes, and combed my hair. Later, Martha could help me into the hospital scrubs I wear for pants these days. Easier to get on over the cast.

Jolie was on the phone a couple of times while I was in the bathroom, talking too softly for me to hear. Not that I eavesdropped, but I wondered how she was describing me to Scoobie and Harry. Because I was fine, he wouldn't come over until at least nine, since that's when the B&B stops serving muffins. But he'd want updates before then.

I drove into the living area and was greeted by Jolie's amused expression.

"How does it feel when you're the trouble maker?" she asked.

Tempting as it was to say I wasn't, I smiled. "About like you'd expect."

I glanced at the food. It was at the head of the table, leaving space for the scooter, but I had to pull up at an angle to the plate. "Gosh, I guess after this I'll have to be sure to transfer to a chair. I can pull a chair up closer."

She nodded. "I thought about that. You can reach, right?"

"Surely." I sat somewhat sideways and picked up a fork.

"I know better than to offer to help. You'll ask, right?"

"I will."

Jolie sat in one of the dinette chairs, facing me. Or as much as one can at a diagonal position. Her hair was pulled back in a scrunchie, and she had on a dark green turtleneck plus a maroon vest with small snow people in various poses.

Unlike me, she is quite short, maybe five-two to my five-six. Jolie sat forward in the chair. She likes her feet to touch the floor.

"So, you had quite a night."

"The only annoying part is that the body was gone when we got back to the laundry room."

She nodded. "I heard that."

I studied her between bites of scrambled egg. "Out with it. You think I was imagining it."

"Not necessarily. You had a reason to go in there. You heard something. Is there, um, any chance there were clothes at the bottom of the laundry bin. Instead of a person, I mean?"

"Clothes that hopped out and jumped into the washing machine?"

"Oh. I hadn't heard it was an empty bin when they looked."

"Except for the man in it, it was empty when I looked in it." I finished the eggs and picked up a piece of toast, on which she had put strawberry jam, my favorite.

Jolie said nothing, but glanced from my toast to the clock and back to me.

"You need to get to a house to appraise, young lady."

She grinned. "It's been a while since you've thrown me out of a room."

"We can't resolve anything. I know what I saw. No one else saw it."

"It's just…I don't want you to think, well, that I don't believe you. You always stick by me."

I forced some humor into my tone. "And a chore

it has been sometimes."

"Do you need anything from the store?"

"How about some Amaretto?"

"Didn't you sign something that said no alcohol in the apartment?"

"Harry signed for me. I never agreed."

She grinned. "Let me try to figure out something." She glanced at her watch. "I wanted to see you for myself. Harry will come over in a bit. If you're okay, I'll head out. I want to get this house done so I can go to the court house Monday to check out comparable sales."

"Better than okay." When she got to the door I called to her. "Tell Lester I like the scooter."

CHAPTER THREE

Scoobie Exercises Patience

AS I PREPARED FOR THE DAY'S first patient, I thought about Aunt Madge. Her early morning sojourn had me really worried. She is the family rock, always the nonjudgmental ear. If she was seeing nonexistent people in laundry bins, it was a bigger issue than if somebody like Melvin was. He already acted as if an x-ray machine gave him a radiation overdose.

Saturdays were quiet at the hospital, usually only emergency patients. The next patient was scheduled, but because of a special request from his doctor.

I glanced at the note in the electronic chart. He was at the hospital because the doctor couldn't figure out why he had regular nosebleeds. They started when he'd been hanging upside down on his father's chin-up bar a few days ago.

The door opened and six-year old Samuel Eugene L. Meyer walked in. He was tall for his age, with tight black curls. He wore a hospital gown over blue jeans and carried a rolled leather belt. His dark brown eyes said the swagger was probably to hide a serious case of nerves.

"Hello, Samuel." I gestured to one of two plastic chairs. "Have a seat for a second."

His mom looked more nervous than he was. I nodded at her and gestured to a spot along the wall as I pulled up the second chair and sat almost knee-to-knee with Samuel. "Heard your nose is misbehaving."

That earned a slight smile. "Yep."

"I'm going to help your doc figure out why. It won't hurt. An x-ray lets the doctor see if the bones in your face are lined up just right."

"No needles?" he asked.

"Not a one." I looked at his mom. "You're welcome to stay, but if you want to sit outside, it's okay, too."

She was very thin, with a worried expression that looked permanent. "I'll step outside and call..." she looked at Samuel, "your dad, to let him know where we are."

Samuel nodded, and she left. He looked at me. "Like he doesn't know."

"Moms are in charge of worrying."

He looked glum. "Mine sure is."

I stood and pointed to the x-ray table. "You'll hop on that table, and I'll put a hard piece under your head. It's the x-ray film."

He glanced at the table and gave me a dubious look. "Table already looks hard."

"It is, but you'll only lie on the table, and the film, for a couple of minutes." I pointed to the x-ray machine itself, which sat above the table. "I'll move that close to your face and…"

"Are you sure it's up there tight?"

I grinned and pointed an index finger at him. "Yep. Bolts are bigger than my finger. Are we good?"

He nodded and stood.

I put a stool next to the table so he could climb on. "Okay, so lie on your back, and I'll put this under your head." I had already placed the film on the table, and gently raised his head and positioned the stiff film plate.

I looked down at him and straightened Samuel's shoulder a little. "What's the L for?"

He sighed. "Leviticus."

"Some people with that name go by Levi."

"When I'm eighteen, I'm getting my name changed."

"Mortimer?"

He grinned. "You're weird."

"Yep. So, remember not to move. I'll step behind that wall and push a button. You'll hear a buzz, and then I'll tell you it's okay to move."

I did several x-rays of various parts of Samuel's skull, two of his face, one focused largely on the bones around his sinus cavity. When I was done, I walked back to him and moved the machine from over his head. "You can sit up while I make sure I did these right, then I'll spring you."

"Do I get to see 'em?"

"Sorry, not from me. My boss looks at them and then sends the results to your doctor."

Once I looked at the third digital picture, I knew Samuel's problem without having to see if my boss agreed. The tiny safety pin had probably been up there since Samuel first started to crawl. Kids usually aim for their mouths but, heck, any orifice works when you're nine months old and exploring.

I GOT OFF WORK at three, and had promised Melvin I'd stop by Markle's Market to pick up a few groceries. Then I would visit with Madge. I wanted to hear about the vanishing corpse in her own words.

This time Melvin buzzed me up, but he didn't open his door when I knocked. "C'mon, Melvin. Open up." Shuffling footsteps told me Melvin was close enough to peer through the peep hole. "You know it's me, you old goat."

The door opened. "Don't talk to your professor like that."

As I first walked into his apartment, I thought Melvin looked better. He had on a loose-fitting orange tee-shirt and grey sweat pants. Nothing he had to button or zip. Then I noticed his arm was in a makeshift sling. If you can call two paisley ties knotted together and tied around a person's neck a sling.

"What's up? Doctor Knight wrapped you tight because you told her yesterday you didn't want a sling. And you look kind of like you hurt more."

"Put the damn milk away and I'll tell you."

I loosened the cap on the milk and placed several cans of soup and a box of crackers on the counter next to the fridge. Melvin was sitting on his brown sofa, hand resting on a chartreuse throw pillow, when I walked into his living room/dining room combo.

I stood still to stare at him. "Doctor Knight put a splint on that finger and now it's loose."

He frowned. "I mighta done something stupid."

Gee, ya think? "Why did you loosen it?"

"It was in the way."

"Melvin, you can take a leak without taking off a splint."

"So you say."

Something told me he took it off for a more physical activity. I took some newspapers off an ottoman and sat to look him in the eye. "I don't really have time to take you back today. Is there someone you can call?" I could make the time, but I didn't want to be Melvin's taxi service just because he'd done something dumb. It could get to be a regular thing.

"Can't huh? I guess I can call my son. Kinda makes him mad when I ask for stuff." His expression was hopeful.

"You can afford a cab. Will Doctor Knight see you?"

"Yeah, her office is closed, but she's meeting me at the prompt care clinic at the hospital at four-thirty. She's not happy about it." He stood. "What do I owe you for the grub?"

"It was only seven bucks. Consider it a get-well present." I had my hand on the door knob and turned to face him. "If you leave it on tight for a few days it'll start to feel a lot better."

He gave me a sour look and waved me out with his good hand.

I jogged across the parking lot, smelling dampness in the air. I hoped it would stay warm enough for droplets to fall as rain rather than sleet. The white stuff is pretty in December, but not for driving, especially when the temperature goes above and below freezing so regularly.

Aunt Madge's apartment door was open, so I rapped and went in. She was in her recliner, casted foot on a pillow and arm only loosely in its sling.

"How's the one-armed driving going?"

She gently waved the casted wrist at me. "Hardly any pain, so I can rest this on the handle bars. I push the lever with the other hand."

I grabbed a dinette chair and swung it to face her. "I stopped at the director's office on the way in. They say they haven't gotten info on what the cameras picked up."

She closed her eyes for a second, then opened them. "Thank you."

"For...?"

"For believing me."

I shrugged. "For my money, there could be several explanations, but one could definitely be someone was in that bin. Somebody not dead, who got out when you left."

She nodded. "That's what I've been thinking."

"With luck, the cameras'll pick up something. Even if they don't, they can't cover every inch every minute."

She leaned slightly toward me, her good elbow on the arm of the recliner. "The person didn't have to go far."

"Seems about fifty yards or so to the closest emergency exit. Did it buzz?"

"They didn't have to get out of the building, just had to hide in someone's apartment."

"Hmm. Yeah, unlocked doors, I guess." This did not sound likely, but I supposed someone could have stayed hidden long enough to leave after the police did. If they stayed out of sight for an hour or so, no one would look at a camera for the time period when the intruder, if there had been one, snuck out.

"I smell rubber burning," Madge said.

I grinned. "I prefer to think of my thoughts as kindling to brilliance."

She smiled, then sobered. "So what should we do?"

We? "Can we do anything before we hear from the security guys reviewing the film?"

"If I go down to the laundry room, people will think I'm nuts."

"And what, it doesn't matter if I go because they already know I am?"

She raised an eyebrow at me, and I stood. "Not sure what to look for, but I'll go. Which hallway?"

"This one. Midway down."

I saluted her and walked into the hall. No one was walking up or down it, so I moved to the middle. The laundry room door was the only one that didn't lead to an apartment.

I knew from the tour Silver Times staff gave Harry and me that there were several industrial-sized washers and dryers at the far end of the building. Staff did laundry for residents, and they used the washer and dryer in the room here to do loads of delicate clothes. Residents weren't supposed to use the machines, but the room wasn't locked. In fact, the knob had no lock.

When the door opened, a light came on automatically. I stepped in and shut the door. Directly ahead were the machines and a small laundry tub. A glance said the water didn't drain into it, so it was mostly a convenience for hand washing, probably. The bin sat in an area straight ahead, but angled into a recess in the wall. Not really an alcove, just a big dent, probably to accommodate heating ducts or pipes.

The room didn't give off any sinister vibes. I glanced behind the washer and dryer. They were too close to the wall for anyone more than Samuel's size to fit there. No tell-tale matchbook dropped by a fleeing almost-dead guy.

I peered into the laundry bin, which was only about three-and-a-half feet high, and wrinkled my nose. The smell of urine was strong, and a slight discoloration was evident at the bottom of the bin. Any staff member would have cleaned that immediately. However, if they and the police had simply glanced in the room in the wee hours, they might not have stuck their nose near the bin.

Maybe someone had been so scared they peed their pants.

When I walked in, Aunt Madge looked at me with an expectant expression. "Well?"

I sat on the loveseat by her recliner. It was angled so visitors would face her. "Know anyone who's incontinent but still spry enough to hop in a laundry bin?"

"If it was just the first part of your question, half of the residents. Why?"

I explained what I'd found, and finished with, "My guess is the stain is as fresh as last night or it would have been cleaned up."

"Definitely a man," she mused.

"Why do you say that?"

"A woman would have gone back to scrub it by now."

I grinned. "A little sexist today, are we?" When she didn't respond, I added, "I think it means someone was in there, but unless we can get the police to check for fingerprints or the person smiled for a camera, it'll be hard to prove."

She shook her head. "I don't want to ask anyone to look harder. I'm trying to remember what I always tell Jolie."

"Mind your own business?"

She laughed. "That's a given. No, just that we can't always know the answers. If someone was in there, they've left. No one has mentioned having anything stolen, so it doesn't matter if I never know."

I stood. "Jolie would never buy into that."

CHAPTER FOUR

Curious Aunt Madge

AFTER SCOOBIE LEFT I transferred to the scooter and headed for the hall. I'd used my lack of sleep as an excuse to ask for a lunch tray in my apartment, because I hadn't wanted a bunch of questions. I couldn't do that for dinner. Or I could, but people would probably stop by to see me. It would be easier to join the others than to talk to five or ten people one-on-one.

A glance at the clock showed only four-thirty, so I didn't go directly to the dining room. I wanted to see where the security cameras were. At least two were trained on the lobby door, but I had no idea where others were.

I turned right and drove to the end of my hall, with only a brief glance at the laundry room door. A camera stared at me from the end of the corridor, at ceiling height. It protruded from the wall a few inches so it could swivel.

The camera was pitifully slow. Even someone using a cane could avoid it by ducking into an alcove midway down the hall.

At the end of the hall, I turned around. Now the camera that faced me was easily thirty yards or more away. It was pointed lower, so I doubted it would reach where I sat. That meant the middle of the hall was only covered by one camera, which would make it easier to avoid being spotted. Still, someone would have to study the cameras to evade detection.

I stopped at the alcove, one of several throughout the facility. Each had a couple of easy chairs, with an end table between them. The day's newspaper was in each one, and a shelf of books stood behind the chairs.

A couple alcoves were big enough for a table for card games or puzzles. When I was more used to the scooter, I'd check out the books.

A final glance up and down the hall told me a person could avoid the cameras fairly easily. But why? No one cared if residents were up at night. A couple residents had early-stage Alzheimer's and paced the corridors after dark. Sundowning, I thought they called it.

I sighed and drove toward the dining room. Perhaps I had scared one of the residents and they had gone into the laundry room to avoid me.

I should probably take my own advice and leave well enough alone.

Lance was ahead of me in the hall, walking slowly.

"Beep, beep."

He turned and shook a finger at me. "You have an airbag on that thing?" He moved closer to the wall so I could ride next to him.

I slowed the scooter. "It's designed to withstand crashes. You doing okay?"

"Just tired. I think Elmira is sweet on me. She dropped by my apartment at seven-thirty last night. In old-people time, that's like midnight."

I laughed. Elmira Washington is to gossip what shells are to the beach. She has a lovely town home on the Silver Times grounds. For a small fee, she can join us for meals, which she has begun doing a few times a week. Lance and I try to get to the dining room early, so we are at a full table for four before Elmira arrives.

Today, we sat with Ed Hardin and his wife, Vicki. I usually don't think of women in terms of their husbands, but Vicki has to rely on Ed for her memory and encouragement to eat. Some residents don't like to sit with them. Conversation with Vicki consists largely of inquiring whether she likes her food. When you ask, she seems surprised to find herself eating.

I don't mind being with them. They used to live not far from me and we all went to First Presbyterian. Vicki often worked in their small garden, and through the years had given me tomatoes from time to time. It's hard to see such a vibrant person losing herself.

Lance pulled a chair away from the table so I could scoot up to it. I was still too far from the table, so he gestured to a staff member to help me into a chair. I silently blamed Lester. As if it was his fault I was in the scooter. I needed to learn to use the walker well enough to get to the dining room easily.

"Thanks." I smiled at the woman who helped me, but couldn't remember her name.

"I'll ride your scooter into the hall, and bring it to you when you're done."

Ed Hardin was wearing a burgundy cardigan and a small frown, but he nodded to me. "No one can say the staff here aren't helpful." Then he muttered, "Can't say the same for…"

I couldn't hear his last word or two as I reached for my cloth napkin. "You feel okay, Ed?"

He moved his silverware from the left to right side of his empty salad bowl. "Just a tad worried."

Lance met my eyes and jerked his head, almost imperceptibly, toward Vicki.

"Can I do something for you, Ed?"

He smiled at me and glanced at Vicki. "No, no. I just need to figure out…some things."

As Vicki looked at a spot on the wall just beyond Lance, Ed continued, "Vicki is getting more dependent on me. Even to…you know, use the restroom. I don't mind, but…"

When Ed paused, Lance looked at me and added, "You haven't been here long. You probably haven't heard the powers that be seem to be getting more strict about how much you have to be able to do for yourself to stay here."

I nodded and looked at Ed. "I heard a bit. I hope you don't have to move."

A voice came from behind me. "Are you moving? I'm on the waiting list."

I stiffened, but didn't turn around. "Evening, Elmira."

Lance nodded, and Ed just looked more miserable. She took a chair from the table next to us and swung it around so she could sit at the corner of our table. I was glad there would not be space to add a fifth plate.

"I'm getting tired of the steps in my townhouse," she said.

I glanced at her. Elmira often mentioned that she walked every day, one reason she kept her steel grey hair so short. From what I could see, she looked as healthy as ever.

"Have you thought about the independent living apartments?" Lance asked.

"Yes, but I figure I'd end up here eventually, so why move twice?"

This made no sense to me. It was easily $1,500 more per month to be in assisted living. Who would spend that kind of money if they didn't have to? "What was the name of the woman from church who lives in those apartments?"

"Margaret Chasworthy," Ed and Lance said together.

"She makes quilts," Vicki said.

I was surprised to hear Vicki say something so cogent. "She does. As I recall she donates one for auction every year, for the First Prez bazaar."

Vicki went back to staring at the spot on the wall.

"So," Elmira asked, "When are you moving?"

Ed's stare was steely. "We hope not to move."

Elmira frowned. "Oh. If you decide…"

"Mrs. Washington, I have a seat for you over here." The staff member who had helped me into the chair was directly behind Elmira.

Before she could object, Lance nodded at Elmira. "Enjoy your dinner."

As she walked away, Ed muttered, "Too bad we aren't allowed to tip the staff."

We were only halfway through dinner when Vicki stood and started for the door that led to the hall. Ed rose to follow her.

"I'll have them put your food in a box and bring it down to you," Lance said.

I watched them walk out, Ed hurrying to catch up with Vicki, and turned to Lance. "He seems able to handle her. Would they really be forced to move to the nursing home?"

Lance shook his head. "No one can make them go anywhere, but the new regime can make them leave here."

CHAPTER FIVE

Madge's Unwelcome Guest

HARRY CAME OVER after dinner and he, Lance, and I played Scrabble for more than an hour. I usually play with Scoobie, who beats everyone in far less time, so I was ready for the game to end when it finally did.

Lance stood to leave. "I need to brush up on my vocabulary."

"Join the club," Harry said.

I picked up the two quarters I'd won and pretended to drop them in my bra. "I'll keep my winnings safe."

Lance blushed as he left.

Harry shook his head slightly, but he was smiling. "You can get booted for lewd behavior."

"I should be so lucky. You willing to make us a cup of tea?"

"I'll grab one from the serving area down the hall. You look at this while I do that." He took a plastic bag from the chair next to him, plopped it on the table in front of me, and grinned.

Inside were three boxes of temporary hair color, brown, blonde, and auburn. I pulled out the blonde. It wasn't my usual brand, but that hardly mattered. I started to read the label.

Harry walked back in and put the two mugs of tea on the table. "I saw they have honey. You want some?"

"Not tonight." I held up the box of blonde coloring, which had a picture of a twenty-something woman with long hair. "You guarantee I'll look like this?"

He stooped to kiss me before sitting down. "I think you're perfect as you are. Jolie thought you might feel more yourself in one of your favorite colors."

I sat the box on the table. "I probably would."

"Jolie's coming over tomorrow, but you'll have to sneak to do it. I guess you aren't allowed to use chemicals like that in your apartment, and I can't see you climbing into a chair at the beauty parlor."

I WAS IN BED, wide awake at two AM Sunday morning. I sat up. "I shouldn't have had that tea." I turned on the light by the side of the bed and gently swung my casted foot across the bed and down. I hated the way it felt when it first touched the floor, but after a few seconds of blood rushing down, the pain abated.

Per my instructions, the scooter was by my bed. I had an appointment with the physical therapist in the nursing home unit later in the day. Thankfully, they had one person on duty on

Sunday, so I could learn to use the walker better with only one useful arm.

No way I was leaving my apartment tonight. I drove from my bedroom into the main room and flipped on the overhead light, which made me squint. Usually I read, but the pain medicine did a number on my powers of concentration, so tonight it would be television.

I settled into the recliner and used the remote to find an old Perry Mason movie. I preferred the good-looking men on NCIS, but the show's owners didn't seem to want to compete with weight loss ads and sixty-year old detective shows.

Perry was doing a biting cross-examination of Lieutenant Tragg when I heard voices outside my door. I muted the TV with the remote and listened. It sounded as if two people were walking farther down the hall. Probably Gina with one of the Sundowners.

I turned the sound back on. Perry had just begun closing arguments when there was a thud against my door. That was far from a normal sound. Maybe someone was hurt.

I surprised myself with how fast I hopped onto the scooter and pushed the help button around my neck. Thank goodness for adrenalin.

It wasn't until I pushed the automatic door opener that I realized the thud was a person. The person who had been leaning against the door was now slowly sliding down it, bringing with her my door's Christmas wreath.

At first all I noticed was the dark green sweater, but then the face became clear. Mrs. Hewlett's final expression was one of surprise.

Probably because she hadn't expected to be stabbed in the chest.

IT TOOK ME SEVERAL minutes to calm Gina, but she was able to speak by the time the police and EMTs arrived. Just like detective shows, they had all put on paper booties, presumably so they didn't add their DNA to the area around Mrs. Hewlett.

No one attempted to revive her. I would have lowered myself to the floor and begun CPR if I'd thought I could help her.

Within fifteen minutes the chief himself, Captain Edwards, was in my apartment. He looked toward the door to the hall. "Morehouse! See if someone can put up sheets or something in the hall, so we don't have gawkers."

He turned to sit on the loveseat, facing me. In a more normal tone, he said, "I'm sorry you can't leave just yet, Madge. I need to let our crime scene people collect evidence and take photos before we move the deceased."

"Sondra Hewlett," I whispered.

"Yes." He stood and walked to my small refrigerator to pull out a bottle of the water Harry keeps in there. I thought he did it for himself, but he unscrewed the cap and handed it to me. "If I had something stronger I'd give it to you."

I managed a weak smile as I took a few sips. "I'd take it. I should probably call my husband."

"The young woman, Gina I think her name was, she did. He didn't answer, probably sleeping. When we get a minute, I'll send somebody over to get Harry."

I waved a hand. "I just want him to know I'm okay." I felt warm tears splash down my face, but I sat up straighter. "I am fine. It was just, just such a shock. And someone I know…"

He sat back on the loveseat, and his questions were clipped. "What did you hear? Why did you go to the door?"

I described hearing voices, but not what they said, and the thud. "I didn't hear a scream, or even a gasp, but I did have the television on."

"And Mrs. Hewlett looked pretty much as she did when we got here?"

I took in a breath. "There was more blood on her clothing by the time you arrived."

His expression softened. "Can you think of anything else that would be helpful?"

"Not just now, but you know I'll call if I do."

As he stood, several familiar voices drifted in from the hall.

"I need to get to her," Jolie said.

"We do," Scoobie added, in a slightly calmer voice.

Sergeant Morehouse said, "Dammit, George, stand back."

Captain Edwards started toward the doorway, and I raised my voice. "I'm fine. Stay there. You don't want to see this."

Jolie's voice was a sob. "Aunt Madge?"

"Call her on the damn phone," Morehouse said. "Get back to the lobby."

My phone rang. It was on the dinette table, very much out of reach. I called out, "Sergeant?"

From the hall, he said, "Get that, would you Dana?"

I had avoided looking toward my door to the hall. I wished someone would use a sheet to hide my view.

Dana Johnson came into the apartment by almost leaping over Mrs. Hewlett. My phone is set to ring six times before it goes to voice mail, and she got it on the fifth. "She's here, Jolie, just a sec."

I put on my best tone of authority. "I'm not going to tell you I'm fine, but I'm certainly not injured in any way."

"Oh, Aunt Madge. I'm so sorry this had to happen to you."

I heard their friend George say, "Ask her who it did happen to."

"Shut up, George," Scoobie said. It sounded as if he was sharing the phone with Jolie. "Madge, I'll go over and get Harry in a bit. You can go home, or stay with us."

I had enough of my wits about me to know I was better off with more people to help me. People who didn't have to go to work. "There is a guest unit here, but I doubt I'll need to move."

After a beat of silence, Jolie said, "I, um, guess that's good."

I tried for a no-nonsense tone, but couldn't quite carry it off. "It didn't happen in my apartment. It happened...she was killed, outside my door. Or near there."

George said, "They'll get the carpet taken up."

"Like that matters," Scoobie said.

George spoke in a low voice, but enough for me to hear. "A lady on the other side of the lobby said it was the woman who runs the place."

"Mrs. Hewlett?" Jolie asked, hoarsely.

I lowered my voice. "Yes, but not everyone may know it, so don't talk about it."

"I'm looking around the lobby," Scoobie said, "I think the word is spreading. People are pretty upset. I think...Hey, there's Lance. He must've heard it was your apartment. I need to go over to him."

"Aunt Madge, I'm going to send George to get Harry."

I heard a grunt of dissatisfaction. George used to be a reporter. He still has the police scanner, and once told me he went to a lot more crime scenes than the woman who took his place at the *Ocean Alley Press*. Not that there are many violent crimes here. George probably wanted to stay in the building, and more likely Jolie didn't want him pressing me for details.

Irritation was apparent in his voice when George asked me, "Should I go to the side door or the front?"

"The side. You won't wake up the guests. I think we have three." Not that George cared.

I heard George say goodbye to Jolie, and realized I didn't know how they got here so fast. "Did the police call you?"

"No. George had his police scanner on, and when he heard a call about a death here, he called Scoobie and me."

"I promise that if I plan to die I'll give you plenty of notice."

From the hall came the sound of wheels on carpet and metal striking metal. A gurney to remove poor Mrs. Hewlett.

Scoobie Offers Counsel

WHEN JOLIE AND I WERE ABLE to enter Aunt Madge's apartment, which she refused to leave, we could tell that, despite her calm expression, she felt anything but. Her hands shook, and she even let Jolie hold the mug for her first couple sips of tea.

She leaned back in the recliner. "There aren't many ingredients in tea, but you'd think it's an elixir for calm."

I couldn't resist. "I read an article that said sometimes there are unlisted items. Like weeds."

Jolie looked exasperated, but Aunt Madge laughed, just for a second. "Whatever it is, I hope it lets me sleep."

"Not that kind of weed, Aunt Madge," I said.

She turned to me as Jolie offered her more tea. "Is Lance all right?"

"Once he heard you were. I walked him back to his apartment."

"Thanks." She shut her eyes for a moment, and then looked from Jolie to me. "Why do you suppose she was here in the middle of the night?"

Jolie hesitated, then said, "I think I heard Gina tell a resident she didn't know Mrs. Hewlett was in the building."

"You think you heard?" I asked.

"Gina was pretty stuffed up, from crying. Then Sergeant Morehouse came over and walked her into the office."

Aunt Madge glanced at the wall clock. "You two need to get home. What shift do you have tomorrow, Adam…Scoobie?"

"Seven AM, but I'll still get a couple more hours of sleep. Won't hurt me for one day."

Jolie stood next to Aunt Madge as she used her walker to get to the bedroom. It took a lot longer than the scooter, but was probably easier than climbing on and off just for a short ride.

"I'm heading out to the lobby," I called.

The lobby was quieter than thirty minutes ago, but no less crowded. The difference was that most of the sobbing residents had gone to their apartments, and the ones who remained were talking to the several nurses and other staff who had come over from the nursing home to comfort people.

Gina was taking a very elderly woman's blood pressure. None of the staff in the assisted living apartments are highly trained health workers. Residents aren't supposed to need much nursing care.

Staff know how to do a few things, like take a person's temperature or blood pressure. As I watched, Gina took off the cuff and squeezed the woman's hand to reassure her.

Dana and Sergeant Morehouse were talking quietly near the entrance, and I walked over to them. "You're sure Madge is safe?"

Morehouse gave a small shrug. "I can't think of any reason someone would want to hurt Madge, or anyone else here." He spoke in a slightly raised voice

I thought his tone was more for the listening residents than me. I lowered my voice. "Why was the director here at this hour?"

"No one seems certain. We'll have the cameras, maybe they'll show something."

Dana's gaze had shifted behind us, and I followed it. A young patrol officer, in a very starched uniform, was coming up one of the hallways toward us.

"What is it?" she asked.

He glanced at me.

Morehouse nodded in my direction. "He's okay."

In only slightly more than a whisper, he said, "It looks as if the exit door closest to where she was found gets propped open regularly. There's a large rock near it, and a thick piece of wood about the length of a ruler."

"Cigarette butts, too?" I asked.

He nodded.

I looked at Morehouse. "I've noticed people smoking out there."

"Staff?" he asked.

I shook my head. "Residents. Staff go outside the main entrance. The door's only alarmed at night."

Dana looked at me. "You here much? Notice anything unusual lately?"

"I'm in and out, but nothing comes to mind." I looked from her to Morehouse. "You should talk to Madge more when she gets up. She never misses anything."

He grunted. "Be here all day, probably."

Captain Edwards called to them, and Dana and Morehouse walked toward him.

I figured Dana was on duty, because she was in uniform. She's in her early thirties, too. Dana took the sergeant's exam not long ago. She passed, but she has to take some classes before the promotion. Jolie kidded her a couple of weeks ago, saying that Dana's clothing budget would go up once she didn't have to wear a uniform.

Morehouse has been on the force about ten years longer than Dana, and he usually wears polyester pants and ties. They go with his short hair to complete a sort of 1960s cop show look. Tonight, he must have grabbed clothes quickly. He was in khaki pants and a blue knit shirt with a Knights of Columbus logo on the breast pocket.

"Scoobie?" Jolie had come up behind me. "You doing okay?"

"Yeah. Really worried about Aunt Madge, though."

The sliding doors opened and Harry rushed in, just ahead of George. He stopped inches from us. "Where is she? Was she hurt?"

I answered. "It was upsetting, but you know how she is."

Jolie gave Harry a hug. "I sat with her briefly after she got in bed a minute ago. I'm sure she's still awake."

Dana had noticed Harry and walked over. She gave him a thirty-second recap of what the police knew, which was essentially only what Madge had told them. Harry only half-listened, but George was all ears.

"Thanks, Dana," Harry said. "I'll head to her apartment."

George glanced around the lobby and back to Dana. "Where's Tiffany?"

"I heard your successor's dad broke his leg a couple of days ago. I think she's in Trenton with him." Her tone lightened. "Your nose must be out of practice."

"Huh." George pulled a notebook from his pants pocket. Even though he's an insurance investigator now, preparing to get his private detective license, it's the same kind of thin pad he carried as a reporter. "Guess I'll cover for the paper. What can you tell me?"

Jolie looked at me. "I'm really beat. I think it's harder when she's hurt than when I am."

CHAPTER SIX

Aunt Madge Ponders Possibilities

I REMEMBERED MRS. HEWLETT as soon as I woke up. The clock on my radio said six-thirty. Harry hadn't left until four, but I wasn't too tired. I was antsy. In twenty minutes my teeth were brushed and I had on a clean top. Good enough for breakfast.

My dinette chairs were spread around the living room from police or others sitting in them, and the light was on over the sink. Probably a staff member had let themselves in to check on me. I looked toward the door. The carpet was in one-foot squares, and several had been taken up. The air smelled of cleanser of some sort. Whatever it was had bleach in it.

It was hard to believe that just a few short hours ago I was thinking about coloring my hair. Something that normal seemed inconsequential now.

My thoughts turned to Harry. He had been distressed that I didn't want to move to another unit, but neither the police nor he could give me a good reason why I should. Bad enough to have to be in an assisted living place, worse to let some maniac force me out of my own spot.

The police were done in my apartment before Harry and Jolie left. I told them just to shut the door as they left. And lock it, of course.

I was just starting for the door to the hall when a key was inserted in the lock and it opened. A woman in nurse's scrubs and a bright pink sweater came in.

"Oh my, I assumed you were in bed. I should have knocked." She flushed. "I was coming in to check on you."

She was in her late thirties or early forties, with brown hair in a French braid. She looked tired.

"How about checking with me in the dining room? I'd like some coffee." And I wanted to get out of the apartment, which suddenly felt cramped.

She held the door open, and walked down the hall next to me. "Have we met?" I asked.

"Helen Hughes. I worked the bake sale table at one of the Harvest for All Fundraisers." She moved her sweater a bit. "Sorry, I was covering my name tag."

"Of course. Thanks for the reminder." The food pantry at First Prez is Jolie's baby, and I usually help at the events. Probably not the next one. "Are you working over here today?"

"Yes."

We had reached the dining room, and I drove near the table where I would sit. "Can I impose on you to move my scooter to the hall after I transfer?"

After she had done that and was back, I gestured to the seat next to me. "We're never full at breakfast. Can you sit for a minute?"

A woman I didn't know, but wearing a Silver Times name tag that pronounced her Sarah, set a thermos of coffee on the table. "I'll bring eggs and toast in a minute, if that's what you would like," she said.

I agreed and turned to Helen. "Do they know any more?"

She shook her head as she poured us both coffee from the thermos on the table. "I know little except that she was found at your door. I'm sorry you had to see that."

"Agreed." The first sip of coffee was just the kick I needed. "Why was she here?"

She glanced around the nearly empty room. "We aren't supposed to talk about it, but as it was your apartment..." She sat up straighter. "No one expected her to be here, but several people said she would drop by periodically just to see how things ran when she wasn't working."

"At two AM?"

"Seems unusual to me, too, but she was pretty dedicated."

"Who will operate our building now?"

Helen stiffened.

Before she replied, I said, "I'm sorry. That sounded thoughtless. I didn't mean it that way."

She relaxed. "I imagine Mr. Renwood, the overall director, will be around a lot until they pick a new assisted living director."

Lance came in and made for our table. He sank into the chair next to me, looking every bit his almost ninety-five years. "I was really concerned about you."

"Scoobie said he walked you back to your apartment."

Lance held up his coffee cup and smiled at Sarah before he said, "Saved me a lot of worry, knowing you were okay." He looked at Helen, who had been quietly regarding us. "I should have introduced myself. Lance Wilson."

Helen gave a tight smile. "Nice to meet you. We were just talking about how dedicated Mrs. Hewlett was."

"Dedicated," I said, "and apparently making some changes. But not the kind she'd be killed for."

"What kind of changes would those be?" Lance knows how I think, so he gave me a look that was half grimace, half grin. "The killing kind, I mean."

I leaned forward. "I certainly wouldn't kill to get in here, but how many people was she trying to throw out?"

Helen's eyes widened. "Throw out?"

Lance stopped smiling. "Mrs. Hewlett was stricter than her predecessor in interpreting how fit you had to be to stay here."

When Helen didn't say anything, I asked, "Wouldn't you rather be here than in the nursing home?"

She stiffened. "Usually we leave decisions on level of care to a resident's physician."

It sounded like a standard corporate line, so I didn't comment. I thought I'd just learned that Mrs. Hewlett's ideas about moving people like the Hardins to the nursing home were not widely known.

MY REMARK WAS NOT popular. However, since a dead woman had fallen into my apartment this morning, the Silver Times administrator was polite when he stopped by after my physical therapy appointment, he was very polite.

Mr. Renwood had been in charge of the entire complex for only a year. Prior to that he'd been the senior manager for the nursing home, the biggest part of Silver Times. As I took note of his jiggling chins and ruddy complexion, I thought he could easily have a stroke and end up as a patient. And he wasn't even old enough for Medicare.

"Finally," he said, "I simply want to assure you that we strongly consider our residents' preferences when we evaluate placement or relocation within the campus."

The pain medicine seemed to be clouding my judgment. "I'm sure you do. Which is why you understand how important it is to seniors to stay in the part of the campus with the lowest amount of urine in the air."

He reddened even more. "I think you'll find…"

I cut him off. "It wasn't a comment about cleanliness. It's simply more pleasant to be in this beautiful building than sharing a room with someone whose faculties washed out with the sand during the last hurricane."

Apparently he'd had enough of me, because Mr. Renwood left almost as soon as the words were out of my mouth.

I was tired. I transferred from the scooter to my recliner and tried to prop a pillow under my ankle. It's not easy to do by yourself when you can only use one hand well. Still, I could move the casted arm a lot better than a few days ago, when the pain in my wrist made me want to keep it in a sling.

A rap on the door jamb announced Scoobie. It was three-thirty. He must have just gotten off work.

"You have a life. You don't need to check on me every day."

He sat on the loveseat. "I'm going to limit it to the days you find dead bodies."

"I'll miss you."

He laughed. "You look a lot better than you did in the wee hours."

"I probably got more rest than you did."

"Was that Mr. Renwood who just left your apartment?"

"Yes. I made the mistake of saying that not everyone liked Mrs. Hewlett's definition of who could stay here." I relayed the conversation at breakfast and Mr. Renwood's reaction to it.

He sat back. "I thought you hated gossip."

"That's not gossip. It's…speculation."

"Whatever you say." He smiled, then grew serious. "I've thought about it all day. It takes a lot of strength to stab someone."

I wiggled my shoulders. "Ugh."

"Sorry, I shouldn't…"

"It's okay. I thought that, too. But unless Mrs. Hewlett came in here with someone, doesn't it almost have to be a resident?"

"Could be," Scoobie said. "But who carries a steak knife with them? At two in the morning?"

"Goodness. All I saw was the brown handle. I didn't exactly stare."

He nodded. "I heard that at the hospital, from a guy who knows someone who was in the ER when she was brought in. I still haven't heard anyone relate her death to the guy in the laundry bin."

I could have kissed Scoobie for believing me. "No one said anything to me about that. It's crossed my mind, of course."

"Have the police been back to talk to you?"

"No, but I wouldn't expect them to. She happened to fall on my door, but that's all I know."

Scoobie glanced toward the door. "They got those carpet squares replaced fast."

"I thought so, too. I really…"

Another knock on the door jamb brought Melvin Hamburg into the apartment. I really needed to keep my door shut for a while.

Scoobie stood. "You look better, Melvin."

He raised his bandaged hand, but it wasn't a brisk gesture. "Doctor Knight splinted it, and she wrapped it more this time."

"Have a seat, Melvin," I said.

"Oh, I can't stay. I just felt bad. I mean, you're Scoobie's aunt and all." Contrary to what he said, he walked to the loveseat, and he and Scoobie sat.

I knew Melvin had been one of Scoobie's professors at the community college. I wasn't sure why he no longer did that. "Thank you. It was a shock, but I'm fine."

"That's good, good." He looked at the floor, then stood and nodded to me. "I'd shake, but neither of us is good at that now."

Melvin walked out.

Scoobie looked at me. "You know him well?"

"No, barely at all. You've been helping him, haven't you?"

"As much as Melvin lets anyone help him. He's an odd duck."

I thought Scoobie wanted to say something else, but he launched into a story about a little boy who had stuck a safety pin up his nose. I knew he was trying to distract me, and didn't mind.

DINNER HAD A MORE normal feel to it. Almost everyone was in the dining room. I'd heard that a couple people had left to stay with children or friends, but my sense was they'd be back.

The Hardins had just settled at the table with Lance and me when Elmira walked in. She was pale, and grazed a chair as she made her way to our table.

"Madge." She grabbed a nearby chair and sat catty corner to our table.

Ed Hardin looked skyward and then began tucking his wife's napkin into her collar.

"Elmira. Do you feel all right?" I asked.

Her eyes widened and brightened as she looked at me. "I'm fine. The flashing lights from the police cars bounced into my townhouse, so I've been awake since about two-thirty. It was your apartment."

"It was the hallway outside my apartment."

"Oh. I thought you'd know more." She looked disappointed. "I wanted to come over for lunch, but they wouldn't let me in."

Lance's eyebrows shot up. "What was the criterion for that decision?"

I suppressed a smile.

Elmira didn't get the dig. "Only residents could come in until just a bit ago." She leaned forward, and spoke in something akin to a stage whisper. "Who do they think did it?"

I shifted in the chair to look at her directly. "Elmira, we've talked through the years about our differing perspectives on gossip. I just don't do it."

She sat up straighter and looked affronted. "It's not gossip. I want to know what happened."

A woman's voice came from behind us. "Are you new here? Would you like to see the evening's menu?"

It was another staffer I didn't know. She was a beauty, with light almond skin and the most perfectly aligned corn rows I'd ever seen. Her ramrod straight posture also implied she suffered no fools.

It occurred to me that none of the staff today were people I knew. It hadn't seemed odd at first, because I've been here such a short time. Perhaps the regular staff had been given the day off to cope with their boss's murder.

Elmira nodded, but she didn't look at the woman. "That would be nice."

"Let me help you to a table, and I'll bring a menu."

Elmira craned her neck to look at the woman, pursed her lips, and stood. "Thank you." She looked down at me. "I'll stop by later."

"I'm having company." I knew I wasn't, but Elmira didn't.

She had no reply. I watched her walk the short distance to a table on the other side of the room. She bumped into the chair before sitting down.

I looked at Lance, who raised an eyebrow. "Early Parkinson's, you think?" he asked.

Ed answered. "I don't see any shakes."

"I guess I don't know all the signs," I said.

"Clumsiness is one," Ed said. "Of course that's sometimes the case with Alzheimer's patients. More a case of being disoriented and bumbling a bit."

Vicki hummed tunelessly as she opened her napkin and dropped a knife to the floor.

Ed bent to pick it up. "Careful, dear."

"She's calm, anyway," Lance said.

Ed frowned as he placed the knife on the other side of his plate. "Mostly. She is getting more fearful, which is also a symptom."

"I'm sorry, Ed." I didn't know what else to say.

Before I could say more, Ed glanced toward the staff member, who was asking people what they wanted to drink. "I wish they'd serve us faster. I can't keep Vicki still that long."

She smiled at him. "I'd like some hot cocoa, with marshmallows."

CHAPTER SEVEN

Scoobie Thinks like Jolie

MONDAY WAS A GLOOMY DAY. At least Aunt Madge had looked okay when I went by yesterday afternoon, and Harry had texted that he thought the same when he stopped by this morning. She even asked him to bring over one of the table-top Christmas trees. She uses a bunch of them to decorate the B&B every year.

I had a nagging concern that whoever killed Mrs. Hewlett would think Aunt Madge had seen something that would implicate them. *I'm starting to think like Jolie. That can't be good.*

"Hey, Scoobie."

Harriet, a nursing assistant who usually worked in the ER, was coming toward me. She helped Jolie with crutches once. Today her expression was drawn and she had dark circles under her eyes. She looked older than her maybe forty years.

"Hey, Harriet. Don't see you much in Radiology."

Her smile was tight. "I mostly work second shift, so I bring people up sometimes in the evening." She stopped a few feet from me. "I didn't realize it was Jolie's aunt who found Sondra Hewlett."

I frowned. "I thought the paper just said she fell outside a resident's door, but didn't name her."

"The *Press* didn't mention Madge. Some TV station in Lakewood did a piece on it this morning, and they did. Sondra was my mom's cousin." She sniffed and pulled a tissue from the pocket of her scrubs.

I'd been about to walk through a secure door to the radiology office. Instead I gestured to a chair in the small waiting area near the mammography rooms. "Gosh, I'm so sorry. I didn't even realize she was originally from Ocean Alley."

She sat and blew her nose. "She wasn't. My mom and she grew up near Philly. Mom and Dad love it here, so she looked for jobs at the shore. Sondra thought she was so lucky to get the job at Silver Times."

I didn't know Harriet well enough to offer a hug. She's usually pretty relaxed looking. Today she seemed stiff, as if she was holding herself together through rigid posture. "Is there something I can do for you?"

She leaned back into the chair and closed her eyes for a couple seconds. "I know Madge, but not well. I heard she's at the place because she broke a leg or something?"

"Ankle and wrist. But she's doing a lot better. Maybe even able to come to the B&B for Christmas dinner."

"That's good. I don't want to bother her, but is there, uh, anything she can tell my mom?"

I must have frowned, because she added, "I don't know her health, would it be a bother...?" Her voice trailed off.

"Not so much that. She's quick to help people. But I was there not long after it happened, and I was at Silver Times yesterday. I might be able to tell your mom something she wants to know."

Harriet whispered. "I think she wants to know if, if Sondra hurt much." Tears ran down her cheeks.

Now I thought it was okay to give Harriet a quick hug.

She sat back and blew her nose again. "I'm sorry."

"No problem." I paused. "Aunt Madge heard a noise by her door, and when she pushed the automatic open button, it was just a few seconds later, Mrs. Hewlett had already passed. I think it happened...really fast."

Harriet drew a long breath. "I think that will help Mom."

My boss, Sam Dent, opened the door to the radiology office. He nodded at me and started to say something, but he noticed Harriet and pulled back in.

"Oh, I'm making you late." Harriet stood.

"I clocked in already. Sam knows if we're talking we have a good reason."

"It's a lot faster pace in the ER." She smiled slightly. "Thanks for talking to me."

"If your Mom still wants to talk to Madge, let me know. I think it would be better than just dropping by."

"Oh, of course."

"Only because it's been hard on her, too."

After more thanks, Harriet walked toward the ER.

It was a busy morning in the ER, which meant a busy time in Radiology. I was in the cafeteria grabbing the cook's infamous chili before I could reflect on what Harriet had said. No one had talked much about Sondra Hewlett, which made sense because she was fairly new to Ocean Alley. I realized I didn't know any more about what had happened the night before last than I did when I left Aunt Madge in what she called the wee hours. Maybe Dana would tell me more.

DANA JOHNSON is Jolie's favorite Ocean Alley Police officer. I got hauled from under the boardwalk or arrested for pot possession enough times that I never hung with cops in my free time. What a difference almost ten years of sobriety and a college degree make. And Jolie.

Dana came out of the locked bullpen area of the department and walked to the front desk. The public area is small, with just a few plastic chairs. No one else was near me, so Dana and I moved aside to talk, her on one side of the counter and me on the other.

She grinned. "Jolie send you down here?"

"Nope. She's so busy running the appraisal business and helping Harry at the B&B, she hasn't been tempted to dig."

"So you are?"

"Not really. We aren't too worried about Madge's safety, it's just...disconcerting."

She was somber. "It is. Since I know you won't blab around town, I'll tell you we don't have a lot to go on."

"Jeez, all those cameras?"

She nodded. "People see TV shows and think cameras cover every inch of a building and hang off of lamp posts so we spot getaway cars."

I nodded. "But you must have something."

She shrugged. "Not much. It doesn't show anyone stabbing her. Usual people were in the hall. The staffer passing out meds, a couple of Alzheimer's patients did laps of the halls. But there was also a person wearing a long coat with a hood."

"You're kidding."

"No. It would have caused the security people to notice if they had eyes on all cameras all the time, but they don't. Silver Times has people monitoring, but there are almost eighty cameras throughout the complex." Dana half shrugged. "Except for a few in lobbies or at main exits, they rotate."

"So, what, they look at them after the fact?"

"If there's a reason to, like now. Otherwise, no. The files are digital, so they keep them stored somewhere for a while."

I drummed my fingers on the counter. "Now I'm officially more worried."

A father and son walked in, and began telling about a stolen bike.

Dana lowered her voice. "If I had to guess, someone wanted to pilfer. We told security out there to change the locks on each apartment. But," she frowned, "I think so far all they're doing is encouraging the residents to lock their doors."

"Great. Rather have another murder than take precautions?"

My voice was louder than normal, and the father looked at me. I gave him a broad smile. "Dana and I are planning a murder mystery fundraiser for Harvest for All."

The father looked annoyed and went back to stating what a shame it was that kids had to have bike locks.

Dana looked at me and lowered her voice as she tilted her head toward the man for a second. "Same philosophy as that guy. Silver Times is going to put more officers on at night. If my parents were in there, I'd tell them to change the locks themselves. Or I'd do it. My bet is whoever was roaming around isn't coming back."

"You think they were targeting Mrs. Hewlett?"

She shrugged. "Nothing in her background suggests anyone wanted to kill Mrs. Hewlett."

The door that led from the back of the lobby to the lot where police parked patrol cars opened, and Sergeant Morehouse came in. He stopped a few feet inside and looked at me. "Jolie send you over?"

Dana gave me a mild eyebrow raise. I took it to mean not to tell Morehouse everything we'd been talking about.

"I'll make sure to remember you to her," I said. "I was going to tell you guys something."

Morehouse walked to the counter and stood next to Dana. "Know anything?"

"Madge hasn't remembered anything else. I don't think she will. Did you know Mrs. Hewlett had family in the area?"

"Huh," Morehouse frowned. "I thought she was from Philly. Her son's making arrangements."

"You know Harriet, the CNA who works in the ER?" I looked at Dana.

"Evening shift," she said.

"I see her sometimes," Morehouse added.

"Sondra Hewlett moved here to be near Harriet's mom, who was her cousin."

"Poor relocation choice," Morehouse grunted. "What's the mother's name?"

I shook my head, but Dana said, "Stewart, I'm pretty sure."

Morehouse frowned. "Doesn't seem like a cousin would know much, but you never know."

I watched Morehouse's back as he walked, muttering, toward the locked door to the police bullpen. I looked back at Dana. "Thought it was better to say that than say you'd been talking about it to me."

"Probably. He trusts my judgment, but you know Morehouse can be prickly."

I did. I decided to drive back to Silver Times. Aunt Madge was probably locking her door, but I wanted to be certain.

CHAPTER EIGHT

Aunt Madge Gets a Confession

I FELT STRONG enough to be up all day, so Lance and I were in the lobby when Scoobie came by about four-thirty on Monday. Lance was on the sofa, but I'd decided to stay in my scooter. Tomorrow I'd try more transfers.

Lance and I were trying to avoid anyone who came by our apartments again to try to get us to play bingo. Not even the promise of eggnog, chocolate Hanukkah coins, or sugar cookies would tempt me.

"You just missed your wife," Lance said.

"It's okay, I'm meeting a date here."

"Yes, you're such a ladies man," I said.

He grinned and sat in one of the upholstered chairs near Lance.

"Just wanted to ch…see you," Scoobie said.

"I'm fine. I'd be better except some TV station said my name this morning, so people keep calling.

Reverend Jamison even came over from First Prez to be sure I'm okay."

We talked about Scoobie's day at work and my growing prowess as a scooter driver. I sensed he wanted to talk about something more important, and he finally said that Mrs. Hewlett had a cousin in town and explained who it was.

"I know Harriet, but not her mother," I said. "But if you think it would help her, I'll talk to her."

"I don't think she'll call," Scoobie said. He looked from Lance to me. "You guys are locking your doors, right?"

Lance nodded. "I think most people are now. I hear the staff using their keys when they pass out nighttime meds."

"What, you listen at your keyhole?" Scoobie asked.

"It's a louder sound than you'd think," Lance said. "I visit my favorite small room several times a night. If they go to an apartment near mine, I hear the lock click."

"Scoobie."

He looked at me. "You like saying my name?"

"I love to see you, but you don't need to come every day."

"I don't feel like I have to. It's just Jolie's so busy."

I raised my eyebrows at him.

"Harry comes," Lance said. "Only problem is if he and I sit with Madge at lunch there's a chair open for Elmira. You want to come at lunch time?"

"Not on a bet. I don't do mean."

From behind us, a man's voice said, "She's not really mean. She's just a pain in the ass."

I turned to look at Melvin. "Recognize the traits?"

Melvin grinned.

"He thinks he's funny," Scoobie said.

I didn't smile. "Perhaps not mean, Melvin, but uncaring about other people's feelings."

"How's the hand, Melvin?" Lance asked.

Melvin had the decency to look uncomfortable, but he ignored my comment. He shrugged and sat in another chair that was part of the lobby grouping. "Don't like the sling. Still pretty sore, but not as bad." He held up his splinted finger. "Looking forward to getting this thing off."

He reached into the pocket of his coat and took out a colorful wooden toy. "Last day of Hanukkah, Madge. I brought you a present."

I recognized the dreidel and held out my hand. Scoobie took it from Melvin and handed it to me. I couldn't imagine why Melvin would bring me a gift.

"You know how to play the game?" he asked.

Before I could answer, the front door whooshed open and Sergeant Morehouse walked in. He did a full stop when he saw us. He seemed to get over whatever surprise he had and looked at me. "You doin' okay?"

"Better. Making any progress?"

"Not a lot. I'm lookin' for Melvin. Heard he'd walked over here."

Melvin was in the process of standing, and his face reddened. "Sure, Sarge, what can I do for you?"

Morehouse gestured to the chair Melvin was in and indicated Melvin should sit down again. Then he sat next to Lance on the sofa, so he faced Melvin.

Melvin didn't sit. "I was just about to..."

"Sit," Morehouse said.

Melvin sat, muttering, "Free country."

"It is." Morehouse looked at Melvin intently. "Did you apologize to Madge for scaring her?"

Lance looked confused, but judging from his straighter spine, Scoobie seemed to understand.

"I never scared Madge!" He looked at me. "Did I?"

"Melvin," Morehouse said.

He seemed to wilt into his chair. "Oh, all right. I'm sorry you thought I was dead."

Lance laughed.

Scoobie didn't. "Don't you mean you're sorry you hid in the laundry bin, scared the daylights out of Madge, and then hoofed it after she saw you?"

Now I could guess why he brought a present. I frowned at Melvin. "At least now people will know I'm not crazy. Why on earth were you there?"

"I was invited over."

Lance had a broad grin. "To the laundry room?"

"No, to visit a lady friend. But she likes to be...discreet."

"I don't care who you visited," Morehouse said. "I want to know how you got in here without being seen. You aren't on any of the cameras until you were leaving."

"Crud. Wouldn't have been on any except for Madge."

I pointed the index finger of my non-casted hand at him. "Excuse me?"

"See," Melvin leaned forward in his chair, "if you know when the camera things move, you can stay out of their aim."

Morehouse stood. "Come on, you're going to walk me through it."

"You tellin' on me?" he asked, as they started toward the hall closest to the independent living apartments.

Morehouse's voice carried back to us. "I don't care who you were visitin' but the people who run this joint might want to know."

"It's not like they let me in..." Melvin's voice trailed off.

When the two men were out of earshot, Lance and I started to laugh.

Scoobie frowned. "If Melvin could get in without showing up on the cameras, anyone could."

Lance sobered. "I'm sure they'll figure out how to keep that from happening in the future."

"What they really should do," I said, "is warn the other women."

Scoobie Scoops George

I LEFT AUNT MADGE and Lance a few minutes later. I had to figure out how to tell Harry that it was Melvin who scared the daylights out of Madge. Calm as Harry usually is, I could see him coming over to tell off Melvin. Jolie would be mad, too, but once she knew Aunt Madge had laughed about it, she would, too.

George's pick-up pulled into the Silver Times lot as I was unlocking my car door. He beeped at me and then walked over.

"So, Scoob, any news about the murder?"

"Morehouse is around. He didn't mention anything. Why do you care?"

"Tiffany has to stay with her dad a few days. I'm freelancing for the paper."

"Thought you still weren't talking to the editor." I looked at George more closely. Since he's been working for the insurance company, he's worn slacks and a dress shirt, occasionally with a tie. This was as opposed to the cargo shorts and Hawaiian shirts he wore as a reporter. "You're still in your adult clothes."

"Funny. I decided to be gracious. You say Morehouse is in there?"

"Yeah. But the story you really want is about Melvin." I grinned as I got in my car.

"Melvin? The guy who retired from the college? What about him?"

"You'll see." I pulled out of my parking spot and headed home. It might seem mean to out Melvin, but almost everyone who knew Aunt Madge had heard the story about her supposedly imagining a body in the laundry room. She deserved to have the real story told.

CHAPTER NINE

Aunt Madge Tolerates a Pest

LANCE AND I WERE alone at our breakfast table when we read Tuesday morning's *Ocean Alley Press*. As soon as George walked into the lobby yesterday I knew Scoobie had alerted him to Melvin's laundry antics. George painted Melvin as someone with an inflated opinion about himself, and a sneak to boot.

There were several hushed discussions, most accompanied by smirks. None of the women was blushing or looked otherwise embarrassed, so either Melvin's companion of that evening was not in the dining room or she had a poker face.

Lance begged off discussion of Melvin's possible friend with benefits, leaving me free to ponder as I finished a second cup of coffee. I told myself I wasn't minding others' business as long as I didn't talk about it.

I said hello to the other residents, but because Lance and I had been friends for years, I hadn't sought much other company. Now, I wished I knew more names.

Heather Broadworthy sat near us. She was in her late sixties. Her husband had started a chain of dry cleaning stores, and they sold it before almost all clothes were cotton and rayon blends. Her husband died a few years ago, leaving her well situated.

However, she'd lost most of her vision, something money can't buy. I'd heard she moved into assisted living not long after breaking two teeth. She bit into a TV remote, thinking it was a bratwurst.

Eleanor and Dave Hampton hadn't been in Ocean Alley long before they moved to Silver Times. They were one of the few married couples in the building, but they never ate together. She usually came to dinner at five, and he at six.

They might simply have different stomach clocks, but perhaps they didn't get along. Eleanor could be looking for a fling, but she wouldn't be able to invite him to their apartment. Unless her husband slept deeply.

The only other women in the room were two friends who called themselves Thelma and Louise. They were really Teresa and Lisa. They played bridge or canasta for hours every day and were constantly looking for partners. It was hard to imagine Melvin at a bridge table.

I thought Heather offered Melvin's best opportunity for wooing. After all, she didn't see well.

Really, unless she was in the hall the night of the murder, Melvin's partner didn't matter. I wanted to know more about how Melvin fooled the cameras. If he could, anyone could.

Lance's comment about hearing keys in the locks didn't reassure me about security. It was a reminder that our apartments were only as safe as the people with the keys. No master key works for all locks, but staff have a big ring of keys with copies of all of our keys.

Gina is smaller than I am. If someone overpowered her, or simply stole keys from the main office, they could get in any apartment.

Idly, I remembered a movie in which some prankster placed a bucket of water above a door, designed to spill when the door opened. What kind of less visible, and annoying, alert could I install? Maybe a net that would fall on an intruder. Or perhaps I could have Scoobie or Harry mount an additional lock.

As soon as I had that thought I rejected it. If Harry thought I was afraid of an interloper, he'd have me home with a private nurse before I could sneeze. I wanted to be home, but not if Harry had to wait on me hand and foot. I chuckled at how literal that thought was.

Instead of contemplating security, I decided to drive through the halls after breakfast. I had to avoid slower residents with walkers, and when I told the activities director I was driving around because I was tired of four walls, she tried to talk me into a crafts session. I had no interest in making felt images of Christmas stockings or dreidels, and it took a couple of minutes to politely decline her suggestions.

It was only when we were done talking that I realized that several of our usual staff were back today. Martha hadn't served breakfast, but I saw her go into the kitchen. She does most of the baked goods, and was probably starting on lunch.

I wondered if Gina would ever come back to work. She was in her early twenties and had a two-year old. Working in a place that had yielded a dead body might seem too risky.

My hallway is to the right of the building entry. I was saving it for last, so I could go into my apartment if I got tired. I started with the hall at the far left end of the building, and watched the camera. It took a full ninety seconds to pan the hallway. You probably couldn't walk the length of the hall without being spotted, but you could go from apartment to apartment ducking into the slight recess at the entry to each apartment. Or going in if one was unlocked. Not comforting.

Camera inspection was interrupted by the physical therapist who came to get me for exercise. Maggie, I thought. I hate to stare at name tags. It's like being eye level with someone else's boob.

Maggie had my walker with her, which meant she'd been in my apartment. I realized that if I locked it regularly during the day, it would be hard to get the scooter close enough to the door to use a key. I didn't like that.

"So, Mrs. Richards, what do you think of your skill level today?"

A loud voice reached us. "Her name is Madge Steele now."

I closed my eyes for just a second, and then turned my head. "I kept Richards, Elmira. I've had the name for almost sixty years."

She had walked beside me by now. "Isn't Harry insulted?"

Elmira had apparently just arrived. I took in her large fake-fur hat and deep brown suede coat, which seemed heavy for a day in the mid-thirties. "No, he's more open-minded than anyone I know."

"Well, if I ever get married again, I'm taking my new husband's name."

"If you do," I emphasized if, "I'll be sure to congratulate you." I turned my head in the direction Maggie and I had been walking. "Good day Elmira."

She stopped walking and turned to go back toward the lobby. "Humph."

Maggie walked next to me in silence for a few seconds. Then she said, "I kept my name, too, and I only had it for twenty-five years."

"Either way is fine," I said. "And I shouldn't have said 'if' so strongly. It was rude."

Maggie smiled. "I used to work at the library. Elmira came in a lot."

It was my best therapy session so far. Maggie changed the height of the attachment I rested my wrist cast on, so I didn't have to bend over so far to use the walker.

"Much easier to use," I said.

She nodded. "I want to encourage you to use the walker as much as you can, but it has to be comfortable for you. I bet you get a walking cast in a few days."

Therapy ended in time for a bathroom break in my apartment before heading to lunch.

Harry stood at the dining room entry, and raised an arm in greeting. When he bent over to kiss my cheek, he whispered, "If you want to avoid Elmira, we'll have to eat in your apartment."

I returned his peck. "I wouldn't do that to Lance. We can stand her for a few minutes."

That proved to be an optimistic assessment.

"Madge," she trilled, "so good to see you."

"It's a beautiful day, isn't it?" I replied.

Harry had just seated himself on my left when Elmira's water glass began to cascade toward him, prompted by her right hand. He jumped up and grabbed one of the cloth napkins to keep the liquid off the seat of his chair.

"I'm so sorry!"

"No problem, Elmira," he said, as she kept apologizing.

Lance and I exchanged a glance as he handed Harry his napkin. I thought Elmira seemed more upset than warranted. It wasn't grape juice or red wine.

"Elmira," I said, "Harry is an old hand with a washer and dryer."

She leaned back in her chair, looking chagrined. "I'm so clumsy these days."

Martha had walked up with more napkins. "Happens every day."

Harry swapped his chair for another one. "I'm trying to teach the dogs to do laundry, but they can't reach the machines."

It was the kind of banter designed to put someone at ease, and it worked. Elmira was soon her busybody self. "I saw the article about Melvin sneaking over here. I bet he's banned."

Lance rolled his eyes at me before speaking. "Most people know Melvin's harmless."

Harry scowled. "Unless he's giving my wife a heart attack."

Elmira leaned across the table and whispered to me. "Who do you suppose he was visiting?"

"Who says he was visiting anyone?" I asked. "Maybe he was taking a stroll."

Behind us, Martha stifled a laugh by pretending to cough. "Mrs. Washington, would you like a green salad or Jell-O with carrots?"

Martha served each of us a green salad and moved to the table next to ours. I glanced around the room. Only three tables for lunch today. It seemed some of the residents who had gone home with children after the murder weren't yet back. I had blocked Elmira, but her voice broke into my thoughts.

"Madge, I asked who you think would have wanted to kill Mrs. Hewlett?"

Harry spoke firmly. "We're having a nice lunch here, Elmira. How about a topic not related to crime?"

"Here, here," Lance said, and raised a glass of Ensure in a toast to Harry.

"So, Elmira, have you decided for sure to move in here?" I asked.

Harry's eyebrows went up. "Why here instead of the independent apartments?"

She waved one hand, as if shooing a fly from her face. "Too much trouble to move twice." She frowned. "But I'm not sure as many people will be moving out now that Mrs. Hewlett is gone."

Harry shot me a questioning look, and I shook my head slightly. Ed and Vicki Hardin were at the next table. I figured Ed was relieved that another director might be more lenient about deciding who could stay in the assisted living building.

"You aren't in a rush, are you?" I asked.

"Just tired of...steps," she replied.

Martha began distributing plates that had the main course, grilled trout with mixed vegetables and a hot roll.

"Martha," Elmira began, "who do you think Melvin Hamburg was visiting?"

Martha pursed her lips for a second before replying. "You don't really expect an answer, do you?" Her tone was clearly designed to cut off Elmira's questions.

Lance had finished his first bite of trout and pointed his fork at Harry. "How are your baking skills coming along?"

"Muffins are no problem. I have, uh," he looked sheepish, "I keep bags of frozen bread in the freezer for the afternoon snack."

I laughed. "I told you that's fine."

He nodded. "Jolie's been trying to teach me to mix yeast and water..."

Lance laughed. "How's that working?"

Harry shrugged. "We don't seem to know the definition of warm water. Or at least it seems to cool too fast."

Elmira left before we had finished our sherbet, citing a need to go to the bank. I hadn't been aware I was sitting stiffly until my shoulders loosened.

"Does she come often?" Harry asked.

"Lately," Lance said, "a few times a week. Not sure why."

Harry glanced at me. "Guess when I come I should grab a fourth on the way in."

"Like golf," I murmured. "She doesn't stay long. Lance and I sit with Ed and Vicki a lot." I looked at their retreating backs. Vicki leaned heavily on her husband.

Lance grinned. "We can always invite Melvin to join us."

Harry's 'no' was firm.

I STARED AT THE CEILING as I tried to nap after lunch. It was ridiculous to let Elmira bother me. Lance and I had the option of asking for a permanent table assignment, but we hadn't because we wanted Harry to join us when he could. Maybe we needed to rethink that.

At least irritation at Elmira kept me from thinking of how Mrs. Hewlett looked when she fell into my apartment.

The phone next to my bed rang and I reached for it. The urgency in Jolie's tone when she said my name made me sit halfway up, leaning on one elbow. "What is it? Are you all right?"

"Yes. Have you heard? Elmira Washington is being held for questioning in Mrs. Hewlett's murder."

CHAPTER TEN

Aunt Madge Ponders the Pest

I COULDN'T NAP AFTER hearing that, so I climbed out of bed and into my recliner. I used the remote to turn on the television, but there was no breaking news item, so I turned it off.

What would make Elmira want to kill Sondra Hewlett? Surely she hadn't come to the building to kill the director. Mrs. Hewlett wasn't usually here at night. Had Elmira snuck into the building and felt threatened when she ran into the woman? But why would Elmira need to be here?

My phone rang again and I reached for the portable handset. Caller ID said who it was. "Hello George."

"Sorry to bother you Madge."

"I doubt that. Are you looking for Scoobie?"

"You, actually." He paused for a couple of seconds. "Did you hear who the police arrested?"

"Jolie called a few minutes ago. It's hard to believe."

"So you, uh, haven't heard anyone talking about it over there?"

"Not a thing." I was mildly amused. George doesn't usually consider me a source.

He sighed. "All I heard was that the police saw someone in a coat with a hood in the halls that night."

"On the cameras, you mean? I hadn't heard that."

"Didn't Scoobie…? Oh, I guess that's not where I heard that. Gotta go, Madge."

I pushed the end button and placed the phone on the lamp table next to my chair. What else did Scoobie know that he hadn't told me?

Before I could so much as open a book, the phone rang again.

Elmira's voice was frantic. "Madge, I'm only allowed one phone call."

I kept my tone formal. "Perhaps you should use it to call an attorney."

"The police did that for me. Madge, I didn't kill her. I was mad at her, but I didn't kill her. You have to find out who did!"

"Just tell the police the truth, it will…"

Her tone became more desperate. "I did, Madge, I did. They, well, they're mad because I didn't tell them I was over there that night."

"Here? At the apartments? Why on earth…?"

Sergeant Morehouse's annoyed voice came through the phone. "Damn it, Elmira, you leave Madge alone!"

Her voice was almost shrill. "I can talk to whoever I want!"

"You said you were calling Reverend Jamison," he said.

I raised my voice so the sergeant would hear me. "Elmira, tell him it's okay if we talk for another minute."

"See?" she said.

"One more damn minute," he said, his voice growing more distant.

"Elmira. Listen to me. If you didn't do it, let your lawyer help you convince the police."

She spoke more quietly. "It's because I had on the hood."

I said nothing for a few seconds, and finally asked, "What were you doing here?"

"I wanted to move in, and she kept telling me there were no empty apartments. I wanted to see for myself."

"At night?"

"I knew that old guy in 281 died last week. I wanted to see if anyone moved into his place yet."

I'd heard people talking about a recent death. While it's not as common as at the nursing home, it happens. No one in the apartments was younger than sixty-five, as far as I could tell. I hadn't recognized the man's name.

"Elmira, there's a waiting list. Surely you're on it."

Her words came out in a wail. "Now they'll never let me in."

Morehouse must have taken the phone from her. "Madge, Elmira has to go. Sorry she called you." He hung up.

I looked at a cardinal on a bird feeder not far from my window, and then at the blank television screen. Elmira had to be pretty desperate to call me. Though she usually seemed oblivious to anything but her own thoughts, she surely knew I didn't like her constant need to talk about others. I'd even told her so directly a couple of times.

Now that I thought about it, I couldn't remember her having friends. No need to wonder why. She must have called me simply because I lived at Silver Times.

I let the leg rest down and stood to transfer to my scooter. Maybe Lance had heard something.

DESPITE HAVING NEARLY all the residents back, the dining room was quiet during supper. Lance and I sat with the Hardins. Harry was coming over for tea after seven.

Vicki Hardin moved the peas around her plate, engrossed in the activity. Ed looked exhausted.

"Ed," I said. "You look really tired."

He shook his head slightly. "Vicki has been awake a lot the last two nights. It's hard to keep her in the apartment."

"They don't mind if you walk, do they?" Lance asked.

"No, but with all that happened..." Ed's voice trailed off.

Lance met my gaze. "Can't believe it was Elmira."

Ed looked up fast, his gaze going from Lance to me. "Elmira did it?"

"So the police say. She maintains she did not." I hadn't even told Lance about her call, though I intended to when we left the dining room.

"Elmira," Ed said, slowly. "Don't know her well. Didn't like her. She hinted to me that Vicki and I should move to the nursing home."

I thanked the staffer who placed a cup of tea by my good hand, and looked at Lance. "How tall would you say that Elmira is?"

Lance raised an eyebrow at me. "Maybe five-three or four. Why?"

"Mrs. Hewlett was taller, I'd guess five-six or seven," I said.

Ed tried to get Vicki to sip her milk as Lance asked, "Why does it matter?"

I started to say because the knife in Mrs. Hewlett's chest seemed to be angled down, but stopped. I supposed if the murderer raised their arm high any wound would appear to be from above. I shook my head. "No point, really. It just seems odd that someone Elmira's size would attack Mrs. Hewlett. And why would she?"

Ed looked up. "Maybe Mrs. Hewlett scared her."

Vicki blew bubbles into her milk and looked up, mustache on her upper lip. "She scares me."

I realized Vicki probably didn't even know Mrs. Hewlett had been killed, and was sorry I had brought up the subject.

"I'm here, pumpkin," Ed said. "I'm here."

CHAPTER ELEVEN

Scoobie on the Prowl

SINCE STAFF CAN USE the hospital's small medical library, I was in there at lunchtime on Wednesday. Aunt Madge wanted to know more about Melvin and Mrs. Hewlett, so I scoured the Internet. We aren't supposed to use the computers for personal business, but no one would know what I printed.

There was little about Melvin. No notice of his hiring at the college, but that wasn't unusual. He wasn't a big-named professor. He had been involved in a car accident five years ago, only noteworthy because the other driver was drunk and had run a stoplight.

"Jeez." Melvin's car had been hit on the passenger side. If he had been hit that hard on the driver's side, he might not be walking around today.

Melvin's retirement reception was announced as a three-sentence mention in the Lifestyle section of the *Ocean Alley Press*. He was said to be leaving to pursue other interests. Dr. Gardiner's wife came to mind, and I smiled.

But, was there more to it? "Pursue other interests" sounded like code for being allowed to retire instead of being fired. I made a mental note to see if anyone knew anything about Melvin's departure. Still, even if he retired before he wanted to, it didn't mean he was anything other than horny when he stole his way into the assisted living building.

Mrs. Hewlett's obituary in a Philadelphia paper had a lot more than the one in the *Ocean Alley Press*. Since she'd lived there most of her life, that made sense. She'd been in the Peace Corps in Liberia just after college, and helped found one of the first assisted living facilities in Pennsylvania. She wanted seniors to have an option between home and a nursing home.

"Don't judge a book by its cover," I murmured.

Aunt Madge also wanted to know if Mrs. Hewlett knew Melvin or Elmira before moving to Ocean Alley. Nothing seemed to indicate that, but newspapers weren't the best way to find out who knew whom.

There were lots of mentions of Elmira in the *Ocean Alley Press*, and a few in the paper in Lakewood. I hadn't realized she used to have a house with a large garden. She'd entered her zucchini in the State Fair and won first place. That was a pretty big deal.

I stopped with my hand hovering above the mouse. The third-place winner was Ed Hardin. Elmira looked triumphant and Ed grumpy. I read the short article more closely. They were both members of a regional Master Gardeners' group. Probably Aunt Madge knew that.

I collected the few articles I'd printed and left a dollar in a large plastic pig by the printer. I smiled. Aunt Madge didn't want to ask Jolie to look because she thought Jolie would give her a hard time about being nosy. I didn't think she would. She'd save the information to use the next time Aunt Madge thought Jolie should mind her own business.

Madge Moves Up on Morehouse's List

IT WAS LUNCHTIME and I was driving my scooter a little too fast toward the dining room before I remembered Elmira wouldn't be jockeying for space with Lance and me.

Lance was sitting with the Hardins, but the usually placid Vicki seemed anxious. I had the walker on the scooter with me, so I parked it at the edge of the dining room, climbed down, and tugged at the walker.

Gina's voice came from behind me. "I'll do that, Mrs. Richards."

I leaned on the scooter's handle bar. "Thanks. Glad to see you back."

Her brow creased, but her lips smiled as she spoke. "It's good to see you." She steadied the walker for me. "I'm here until nine. I'm a little, um, nervous, about working overnights for now."

I put one hand on the walker and rested my casted arm in its holder. "Don't blame you. It sounds as if, well, maybe we can rest easier."

She shook her head. "I don't believe Mrs. Washington did it."

"Really? Stop by later and tell me why."

Vicki's voice reached us, and she sounded insistent as she stood. "But I don't want to."

I called to her. "Do you like blueberries, Vicki?" I hopped toward the table, and Lance stood to hold my chair.

She looked at me, initially appearing suspicious of something, and then her expression cleared. "I like you." She sat.

I smiled at Vicki as I sat. "I like them, too. I'm glad they're on the menu today." I wasn't really, as they would be frozen blueberries. But they're supposed to keep we seniors healthier, so I would eat them.

Vicki was staring at her favorite spot on the wall. I glanced from Lance to Ed. "How is she?"

He shrugged without looking at her. "Hard to know. Yesterday she knew who I was, today she doesn't and is agitated a lot. Doc's going to look in later. Maybe he can increase the dose of this new medicine he put her on."

"I can't assist much, Ed," Lance said, "but if it helps to have someone stop by later, I can do that."

"It's supposed to be almost forty today, so after lunch Gina's going to walk with us outside for a few minutes. Vicki loves that."

"I don't like her," Vicki said.

"Gina?" I asked.

Vicki stared at me and then reached for one of the packs of crackers that always sit in a basket on the table.

"Gina sometimes brings Celia McCarthy to walk with us," Ed said. He glanced around the room. "She's gotten a bit…determined lately."

"Determined?" Lance asked.

Ed nodded. "Sometimes," he lowered his voice, "Alzheimer's patients have a personality change. Celia nudges Vicki if we don't walk fast enough."

"What does Gina say about that?" I asked.

Ed looked up from the package of crackers he'd been trying to open for Vicki. "Celia's smart. She doesn't do it if Gina's next to her."

"I really don't like *her*," Vicki said.

LUNCH HAD BEEN OVER for more than an hour and I was trying to talk myself into walking in the hall with my walker. Moving around my apartment had gotten easier, and it seemed as if the hall would be a good challenge. Finally, I decided that I might get halfway to the lobby and get tired of hopping.

I transferred to the scooter and took a sweater from the back of my recliner. It was forty degrees and cool. Very mild for nine days before Christmas.

I would go outside on my own for five minutes. My goal was go see where the exterior doors were. I knew where they were inside the building, but didn't really know where they led to outside.

As the main entry doors automatically opened, a voice behind me called, "Madge? Where are you off to?"

I turned to see Martha standing near the office. "Just getting fresh air for a couple of minutes. I'm good on my own."

"Do you want a coat?"

"I'm going to ask Jolie to bring me one. We didn't think of it when I was indoors only. I'll be okay for a couple of minutes."

Though she frowned slightly, Martha just nodded and turned to walk toward the dining room.

I drove onto the sidewalk, near the circle driveway. "Brr." Even with a sweater it was cold, and probably felt more so because I'd been indoors for days.

A wide sidewalk wrapped around our one-story building, and I drove toward the back. Since there are only thirty-five or forty apartments, the building was less than half a block long. "I wonder why there are no doors along the side?"

There were two at the back, one at each corner. I studied them and frowned. Just typical metal exit doors, with no automatic openers. That meant residents would have to be able to push hard to get out if there were a fire. "Ugh."

The door near me was also closest to the independent living apartment building. A couple of cigarette butts were on the edge of the sidewalk. Sitting in a small evergreen bush was what looked like a metal coffee can. Probably where smokers tossed their butts. Smoking was not allowed anywhere on the campus. It was hard to imagine staff risking their jobs for a puff, but you never know.

A man's voice came from behind me. "Madge, what the hell you doin' back here?"

I jumped and turned my head. "Sergeant Morehouse. You scared me."

"Saved you from hypothermia more likely. Come in with me." He turned and stood so I could ride next to him as he walked. In his tan trench coat, he was definitely more appropriately dressed for the temperature.

"I haven't been outdoors in ten days, except for the ambulance ride from the hospital to here."

"So you went outside in a sweater and rode toward the dumpster?"

It was an effort to keep my teeth from chattering. "I hadn't noticed it was back there."

Morehouse snorted. "You wanted to check out those doors. I thought you were more sensible than that."

We had reached the main entrance and I rode in ahead of him. "It's good to know all the emergency exits." I saw Martha and Gina halfway down a hallway. "Sergeant, come down for tea."

He was clearly amused. "Bring your kettle?"

"Drat." I stopped the scooter near the self-service drink area. "Make one here. For that matter, make two and you can carry mine."

He put the notebook he carried under his arm and picked up a mug. "Want anything in yours?"

"A bit of honey if they have it."

"Yes, ma'am."

"If you were Scoobie, I'd swat your elbow."

He had finished putting hot water in the mugs and was adding the teabags. "You'd spill the drinks. Go on ahead. I'll meet you at your place."

I pushed the door opener and made for the recliner. A comb and lipstick were in a pocket on the side. I didn't need a mirror to know I looked windblown. Luckily, I could reach the pocket without getting in the chair.

Morehouse came in and set the mugs on the table. He smiled as I put the comb back in the pocket. "Madge, I've seen you after you've been running the bake sale all day at Talk Like a Pirate Day. You have no secrets."

His comment relaxed me. I had felt like a schoolgirl caught sneaking a smoke. "That's true."

"And in your Wonder Woman costume last Halloween."

"Okay, you've made your point." I gestured to the table, and he pulled a chair away so I could drive the scooter close to it. He sat and picked up a mug, blowing on the steam.

I didn't give him a chance to take a sip. "Do you think the door closest to the dumpster is where someone came in that night?"

"When I'm with you and Jolie, I need to kick the idea that I'm the one askin' the questions."

I smiled as I picked up my mug. "Sorry. Were you looking for me?" I knew he'd answer my question eventually.

"More Gina. Didn't talk to her much that night, except for the basics."

"Poor woman. She thought she had an easy job. Or at least a safe one."

"It's never easy to see someone who's been murdered." He set his mug back on the table. "You said you heard a thump at your door, I think that was your word."

I nodded. "And I mentioned hearing low voices a few seconds before."

"But not what they said, right?"

"Correct. I couldn't really tell how many people or if they were men or women."

"You said you had your TV on. Why were you up? Something wake you?"

"No, just had a hard time sleeping the first few days I was here. It's better now."

He glanced around the apartment. "How long you stayin'?"

"I could probably go home now, but Harry would have to do so much for me. And we'd have to widen the door to the bathroom in our bedroom. That would get drywall dust everywhere."

He shook his head slightly. "Madge the carpenter. Built any dog houses lately?"

"Do you think the murderer came in one of those back doors the night Sondra Hewlett was killed? Did you see anyone on the security cameras?"

"You don't think it was Elmira?"

Much as I disliked her, it was hard to imagine her plunging a knife into Mrs. Hewlett. "Why would she have even been carrying a knife?"

"Good question. She is a suspect. She snuck in dressed so she couldn't be identified on the cameras, and then conveniently forgot to mention she was in the building that night."

"But not your only suspect?"

He pointed an index finger at me. "You're worse than Jolie."

"Don't be insulting."

He smiled. "I get your interest, and wouldn't tell you anything to compromise what we're doin'." He shook his head slightly. "No other suspects. She was designated a person of interest, but the formal charge so far was for criminal trespass. We supported letting her out on bail."

"How much?"

"She hasn't got much, so judge made it $50,000. She don't really have anywhere else to go."

"That's sad," I mused.

His expression was shrewd. "Everyone else wants her gone."

"Oh, I do, too. If she moves in here, Harry and I will widen that door." I paused for a moment. "It just doesn't make sense that she wanted to move in here so badly, but came in with a weapon and murdered the director."

"I hear you."

"Melvin knew how to get in."

He laughed. "Melvin's lucky he don't get thrown out of the other building. You're full-up here, but there's vacancies in the independent place or I bet he'd be out on his butt."

"Did you see those cigarette butts?"

"We did. Scoobie said he'd seen residents out there, but no staff."

"Hmm." I studied the clock above the sink for a second. "Staff would probably be more conscious of security. More careful about locking the door when they came back in."

He nodded, smiling slightly.

"You know, during Watergate, those political hacks taped a door so it didn't lock. Maybe the woman Melvin was visiting did the same."

His smile vanished, and he stood. "Thanks a lot for the tea. Tell Jolie I said you're gettin' up there on the pain-in-the-ass list."

I watched the door close behind him. It sounded as if the police hadn't looked closely enough to check for tape residue. Maybe I could get Scoobie to ask Dana about that.

CHAPTER TWELVE

Aunt Madge Keeps Them on Their Toes

I NEEDED TO GO to therapy. I didn't mind going, but I had other things to do Thursday morning. Plus, I hated waiting. Maggie had brought me to the PT unit in the nursing home building only to find someone else using the pulleys she planned to have me use to strengthen my good arm, as she called the one without the cast.

For a time I simply watched the stationery bike riders and tried to guess how much some of the barbells weighed. I soon lost interest in these activities and looked at the magazines in a rack on the wall next to me. All about Hollywood people. No better than gossip magazines.

That reminded me of Elmira, and I wondered what Scoobie had found yesterday. He was supposed to come over before starting to the hospital for his short-shift day, at eleven.

A breathy woman's voice came from my left. "Madge. I heard you were here."

She was about fifty-five and also attended First Prez, but I didn't know her well. I assumed she was here as an outpatient. "What brings you here? You look healthy as a horse."

"I had a mild heart attack a few weeks ago, so I'm doing some cardiac rehab." She hoisted two small weights, one in each hand, above her head, and smiled.

"I'm sorry I didn't know to send a card. When I have several B&B guests I don't always make the service."

She sobered. "I'm glad your fall wasn't worse, and very sorry you found that body outside your apartment here."

"Thanks." I didn't know her well and wasn't sure what else to say.

"Pretty strange about Elmira, don't you think?"

I shrugged. "I don't believe she did it."

The therapy area grew quiet. One of the younger physical therapists, who looked about fifteen but was probably a recent college graduate, had stopped mid-motion in cleaning a therapy table. All eyes in the room were on me.

I made an exaggerated shrug. "Well, I don't."

A man on one of the two bicycles asked, "So, you think a murderer is still walking around?"

WHEN HE DROPPED by my apartment about ten-thirty, Mr. Renwood asked whether the physical therapy appointments had me feeling "as good as new."

I took that as code for "would you please go home."

"The therapists are very good. I can't wait to be fully confident when I transfer to the toilet."

That got rid of him.

Scoobie walked in less than a minute later. "Is it my imagination, or was Mr. Renwood walking out of your apartment looking steamed?"

I leaned back in the recliner. "If I were Catholic I would cross myself when that man comes in."

"You want me to ask Father Teehan to stop by?"

"No. I think the good Mr. Renwood is annoyed that I made a comment in PT today."

Scoobie raised an eyebrow.

"Well, I don't think Elmira did it. And Sergeant Morehouse seems open to other possibilities. I can't help it if some old man thought it means a murderer is still walking around the campus."

"Surprised it wasn't black smoke coming out of Renwood's ears." Scoobie sat on the loveseat and removed several photocopy pages from where he had tucked them in his waistband. "Did you know that Elmira knew the Hardins pretty well?"

I shrugged. "I expect she knows them from church."

Scoobie handed me one article. "And from state fair competition."

I scanned the page. "I remember her talking about that blue ribbon. She didn't mention Ed." I handed it back to him. "That could give Ed motive for offing her, but not for her killing Sondra Hewlett."

Scoobie spoke almost to himself as he handed me the other papers. "Offing her?"

I read without speaking for almost a minute. "I had no idea Mrs. Hewlett had worked in the field so long. But I don't see anything here that indicates she had enemies."

"Me either. Only interesting thing was it looks as if Melvin might not have wanted to retire when he did. But, who cares?"

I handed the articles back to Scoobie. "You can toss these. Or, would you? I don't want them in my trash can."

He took them and folded them in half. "So, are you done wondering about all this?"

"I want to know who Melvin was visiting."

"Not going to be in the paper."

I sighed. "Probably not."

I HAD JUST GOTTEN in my scooter to ride to the dining room for dinner when someone rapped on my open door. "Come in."

Melvin Hamburg stood there, but his neck was craned, looking down the hall.

I stared at him for a moment, and when he looked at me, I asked, "Aren't you banned or something?"

"Technicality. Can I come in?"

His posture reminded me of a kid being sent to the principal's office. "For a second. I was about to ride to the dining room."

He took off a Yankees ball cap and held it in one hand. "Thing is, I didn't really apologize to you. You know, about scaring you and all."

That softened me up. "I appreciate you saying so. I think the *Ocean Alley Press* article was enough admonishment."

He frowned. "Not according to my mother."

"You have a *mother*?"

He grinned. "Everyone has one. Mine happens to still be alive. Surprises people."

"I shouldn't be surprised. I bet she's about my age. Where does she live?"

"A good ten years younger, probably. In Patterson."

I am proud of the fact that I'm in my eighties, even more that I look somewhat younger. Sometimes people think Jolie is my niece instead of grandniece. However, knowing that someone in their mid to late-fifties had a mother younger than I was made me feel my age.

"Sit down for a minute, Melvin. I have a question for you."

He looked almost longingly toward my door, but ambled to the loveseat and sat.

I turned my scooter to face him. "I'd love to know how you snuck in here that night. And how you stayed hidden from most cameras."

He narrowed his eyes, seemingly suspicious of me. "Morehouse tell you to ask me?"

"No. Why would you think that?"

"Thought he might be comparing stories."

I stared at him. "That's why the truth comes in handy."

"Door closest to my apartment building." He looked away.

"Which is usually locked. Who left it open for you?"

He sat up straighter. "Who said anyone did?"

"You might be good at evading cameras, but if someone let you in, they'd likely be seen."

"Humph. It's not all that hard. Those cameras make slow turns."

I already knew that. "You're avoiding the question."

"I can't say who, Madge. They're already mad as hell at me."

They? "Then just tell me how you were let in. I looked at that door. There isn't a place for a key on the outside knob."

"Yeah, that's been a problem."

"Melvin."

"Oh, okay." He looked toward my open door again. "See, you stuff a wad of paper in the recess in the wall, where the thingy on the door goes in. You can't use gum. Then you put tape over the paper and the door doesn't lock."

"But doesn't it set off the alarm?"

He leaned forward, looking very pleased with himself. "See, it isn't alarmed during the day. If you fix the lock before they set the alarm at eight, then it doesn't ding when you open it."

"Does it still work like that?"

He shook his head. "They got onto me. Saw the maintenance guy looking at it. Far as I know it's fixed so the alarm works like it should."

As far as he knows?

I had been about to ask him another question when a man's voice came from my doorway. "Melvin! You know you aren't supposed to be in this building."

I turned to face the young security guard who now walked through the building a few times in the evenings. "Oh dear, I didn't know that. I asked Melvin to come over."

He looked close to incredulous. "You did?"

I thought fast. "I felt he deserved the chance to apologize for scaring me in the laundry room that night."

Melvin was quick to agree. "See, I didn't really apologize right the day Morehouse talked to me."

The guard looked from Melvin to me. "I agree with you, Mrs. Richards, but I'm going to have to escort Melvin to the door."

"Of course. I'm sorry...I don't think I know your name."

He smiled as he gestured to Melvin to come toward him. "Paul. Paul Kieffer."

Melvin winked as he walked by me, but I didn't think Paul saw him do it.

CHAPTER THIRTEEN

Aunt Madge's First Outing

THERE ISN'T TOO MUCH to investigate when you're in an assisted living facility, but I did my best over the next three days. I thought knowing Melvin's paramour could make a difference. Perhaps she was angry if Sondra Hewlett found him sneaking around and ordered him out of the building.

Of course, it would have to be someone able-bodied enough to swing a knife into the director's chest. That left out easily half of the women in the building.

If the woman were a smoker, people would be used to seeing her near the door. Someone regularly seen there might have an easier time stuffing the paper in the lock hole without arousing suspicion.

Then I remembered Melvin had said "they" were already mad at him. Since I could hardly imagine, in fact would rather eat spoiled clams than imagine him in a *ménage a trois*, my guess was the two women didn't know about each other.

While I didn't know everyone who smoked, two women who did, Teresa and Lisa, seemed to walk slowly. They'd probably blown their lung capacity. How much strength would they have to stab someone?

Of course, the official policy was no smoking anywhere on the campus. I'd heard a nicotine addiction was much stronger than alcohol or most drugs. If Mrs. Hewlett told someone not to smoke, it might enrage them enough to provide strength to stab her. *At two-thirty in the morning?*

Thinking wasn't helping.

JOLIE AND SCOOBIE CAME by Sunday morning to take me to church. The sky threatened something wet. I hoped the temperature stayed above freezing, at least until I was back at Silver Times.

I love my First Prez community. The red bricks and white steeple look kind of stodgy, but we are a welcoming group. Several people in the congregation, including Lance, were my rocks when my husband Gordon died more than twenty-five years ago. And it's where Harry and I met. Just driving there today made me feel better.

It was my first outing. We left earlier than normal for the ten o'clock service. Scoobie was going to drop us at the side door to the church, the one with a flat entry and automatic door opener. Jolie and I would go in to find Harry, whose job was to secure a pew near the door. Scoobie would join us.

I hadn't planned on Elmira waylaying us.

She hurried toward us, dragging her coat. "Madge, I knew you believed me."

Word gets around.

She beamed at me. Jolie telegraphed a questioning look as Harry walked toward us.

I regarded Elmira closely. Her steel-gray hair was mussed and the dark purple suit she wore had what looked like a milk stain on the front. "Why don't you stop by this afternoon?"

Harry gaped.

"Aunt Madge," Jolie began.

Elmira almost wailed. "I can't. The only place I can be on the campus is my own townhouse."

There were so few people in church this early that her voice bounced around the pews.

"Calm down, Elmira," Jolie said.

Scoobie walked in as her eyes filled with tears and she said, "No one likes me."

He stood next to her. "You're fine, Elmira. You can sit with us in the community room, after the service."

She smiled through tears. "Oh, I like the doughnuts."

She turned and walked toward the third pew on the left, her usual seat.

The four of us exchanged glances, and I said, "I need to sit."

"Of course," Harry said. "Sorry." He walked the few steps to the pew with me, and folded my walker after I was seated.

"Thanks, honey." When he sat next to me I put my head on his shoulder for a second.

Jolie and Scoobie sat behind us. I turned. "Why aren't you in this pew?"

Scoobie grinned. "I want to keep an eye on you."

Jolie rolled her eyes. "Let me know when acting your age kicks in."

Harry turned to Jolie and spoke quietly. "What's going on with Elmira? She looks a bit...unhinged."

Jolie shook her head, and I spoke in almost a whisper. "Lance and I are wondering if she has Parkinson's."

"But that doesn't affect your thinking," Harry said.

"Not often," Scoobie said. "But it can for some people. I think she's mostly just out of her mind with worry."

Scoobie Helps Elmira

I WATCHED THE BACK OF AUNT Madge's head throughout the service. Reverend Jamison's theme was rebirth. He talked about how it's never too late to decide to live one's life differently, and that Christmas is a time to start anew.

Jolie leaned into me. "A good time to talk about births."

I squeezed her hand. Jolie and I had been on the way to have dinner with Aunt Madge and Harry the night Aunt Madge fell. We had a lot of good news to share, including a wedding date. We'd put the conversation on hold for a few weeks.

The delay changed nothing about our feelings for each other.

Jolie had asked her sister Renée if she minded if Aunt Madge was her matron of honor. She didn't, and they had even joked that since she filled the role for Jolie's first wedding, maybe Renée was a jinx. In any event, Aunt Madge's duties, yet unknown to her, can be done from a walker, but would have been tough from a hospital bed.

It took us a while to get to the coffee klatch, as Aunt Madge calls it, because twenty people wanted to say they were glad to see her. Finally, Reverend Jamison came over and said he wanted her to get a doughnut before the rest of us scoffed them all.

He walked on one side of her and Harry on the other, so Jolie and I strode ahead to secure one of the card tables. It turned out that Elmira was guarding one for us. She had three doughnuts and a bear claw on a paper plate, and a mug of coffee in front of her.

No one sits alone at a church event. She may have shooed people away, but it was also likely that she was being ignored. Even people at the closest table had their chairs angled away from her.

"I don't get this, but I'll get us coffee," Jolie murmured, and walked to the serving table.

I nodded and smiled at a few people as I grabbed a fifth chair for Elmira's table and made my way to her. It's Aunt Madge's church, so I don't know names unless they've helped at Harvest for All. When I was in high school I traveled among the town's churches. On Sunday, First Prez was one of my favorite churches because they had the best food after the service.

Madge and Harry came in with Reverend Jamison. She must have told him who they would be sitting with, because he made a beeline for the coffee and didn't move to join us. My guess was Elmira had been crying on his shoulder for days.

Aunt Madge looked tired now, so people called greetings or waved, but no one encouraged her to stop to chat.

I held Aunt Madge's chair as Harry helped her pivot into it and placed her folded walker against the wall.

"Thank you Madge," Elmira said, in a meek voice.

"I know you've had a tough week. But you have to promise, no gossip."

Elmira nodded. "How did you learn to use that walker with only one hand?"

"It's not as hard as it looks, especially now that the doctor said that I can put my foot on the floor instead of hopping."

Elmira started to say something, but Aunt Madge cut her off. "If you didn't hurt anyone, I don't want you to be accused of it, but I can't help you unless you're 100 percent truthful."

She nodded. "The thing is, I don't know much." She looked at Harry and me, and glanced toward Jolie who was making her way toward us with four coffees on a tray.

I stood to take the tray from her and hand out the mugs.

Jolie nodded at Elmira. She is no fan, because Elmira told half the town that Jolie's ex-husband had embezzled money from his bank.

Elmira kept her gaze on Aunt Madge. "I already told you I wanted to see if that apartment was vacant. I thought Mrs. Hewlett was lying when she said they'd already found a tenant after that man died."

Madge nodded, but it was Harry who spoke. "We could probably find some people to help you get moved into the independent living apartments."

She hesitated. "I don't want to move twice." She smiled wanly. "And I can't move anywhere now. But thank you."

I sensed Aunt Madge's impatience. She looked as if she wanted to be done here and back to her recliner. I didn't blame her.

Elmira took a sip of her coffee. "A lot of people were in the hall that night. I mean, a lot given how late it was."

"Who besides you?" Aunt Madge asked.

"Of course, Vicki and Ed were walking. And I don't know the name of the other woman."

"Celia, probably." Aunt Madge looked at Harry. "I think she has early Alzheimer's, too. Lance says she walks a lot at night."

Elmira nodded. "I heard the front door slide open. That meant it was someone who knew the night code. I kind of hid in the entrance to one of the alcoves, not the one near you, and looked out. When I saw Mrs. Hewlett coming down the hall a minute later, I hid behind one of the chairs."

"Not a lot of space there," Jolie said.

"True, but the light was off, so I thought someone would have to walk into the little room before they'd see me."

Aunt Madge nodded, and Elmira continued. "She was by herself. She walked down to the exit door to make sure it was locked. When I saw that, I hid again. She walked back to the lobby, but I didn't hear the front door slide open, so I stayed where I was."

"Did you see Gina?" Aunt Madge asked.

"She went into an apartment near the TV room. I guess she was still there."

"How long was this before Mrs. Hewlett was stabbed?" I asked.

"Not long at all, I think. I tip-toed to the lobby and looked around. When I didn't see her, I left. It wasn't ten minutes before I heard the ambulance." She put a hand on Aunt Madge's. "If I'd been there, I would have helped."

Rather than just push Elmira's hand off, Aunt Madge used hers to reach for a glazed doughnut. "But why not tell the police you were in the building as soon as you knew what happened?"

Elmira shook her head. "I was scared. Besides." She paused for several seconds. "I didn't want to get Melvin in trouble."

Aunt Madge's tone was sharp. "And why not mention him?"

"After I started having lunch with you, I was in your building a lot. I heard Mrs. Hewlett tell Gina and Martha to call her anytime they saw him in the building. Unless he was paying for a meal."

"No worries there," I said.

She smiled slightly. "Melvin was in my high school class. And he always congratulated me when I won prizes for my zucchini. I knew he wouldn't hurt anybody, but if he did something accidentally..."

Aunt Madge frowned. "I hope you eventually told everything you could think of to the police."

I thought Elmira's expression said she had not. I leaned closer to the table. "Do you know why Melvin retired?"

Elmira nodded. "I think so. He didn't want to. Did you know about his car accident?"

I nodded, but Jolie and Harry said no.

Aunt Madge said, "I have a vague memory of it. He wasn't too badly hurt, was he?"

"He had a bad concussion." Elmira nodded to herself. "He got a lot better, but he still has some troubles. I think he forgets things. A few times he forgot to go to some classes he was supposed to teach."

In my mind, knowing Melvin had memory problems was something to consider. But none of what Elmira told us really reduced the chance that she had committed the murder. It simply meant she spun a good yarn.

We spoke for another couple of minutes, with Elmira asking Aunt Madge, twice, to find out who really killed Sondra Hewlett. Jolie raised a napkin at her mouth to hide a smile.

I began to gather used napkins and mugs. As I held Aunt Madge's chair, I thought of another question. "Elmira, did you get in with the security code at the main door?"

Elmira shook her head. "Melvin told me how he rigged the back door. But he must have left before I did, because it looked like it was locked when Mrs. Hewlett checked it."

AFTER HARRY, JOLIE, AND SCOOBIE left, I sat in my recliner and thought. I needed to think, and I was also too tired to do anything else.

Elmira's comment about what I now thought of as Melvin's door had led me to ask Scoobie to check with Dana about whether they had seen tape on the door. My guess was that Sergeant Morehouse would not tell me. If the police knew the door was unlocked a lot at night, it could change the focus of their investigation.

Who would have been wandering around at about the time Mrs. Hewlett was murdered? There were at least several people -- Ed and Vicki, Elmira, probably Melvin.

What about Celia? No one talked much about her. She was in good physical health and always pleasant. I wouldn't have known she had early-stage Alzheimer's if I hadn't been told. She might have the strength to kill Sondra Hewlett, but what threat would the director have been to her? Maybe she heard talk about transitioning people to the nursing home. That certainly worried Ed.

Gina was on hand, of course. She would be in the office or distributing medicine. Gina said she hadn't seen Sondra Hewlett. But if the director was checking how things worked at night, she probably didn't want Gina to see her. Mrs. Hewlett would know the routines, including how to stay away from Gina as she did her work.

Hallway and other lights are dim at night. Mrs. Hewlett would have had a key to any locked rooms, such as the kitchen or a big utility room that held excess supplies and the recycling bags. Elmira thought she heard Sondra come in the front door, but the director might have been elsewhere in the building. Maybe the door opened for the murderer.

Much as I disliked her, I couldn't see Elmira as a killer. Why would she have been carrying a steak knife? Could she have stayed calm enough to leave the building without being detected? I thought not. She'd been on some cameras at some point, but if she'd been seen wielding so much as a nail file she probably wouldn't be out on bail.

Could someone else, someone who knew the security code, have known that the director would be in the building? Some staff were upset at the schedule changes Mrs. Hewlett had begun to implement, but murder for different working hours? It seemed unlikely.

The building, the entire campus, was safe. However, the one time of year when Ocean Alley had a rise in petty theft was the holiday season. People want money for Christmas gifts, or they simply want to treat themselves because it looks as if others have a lot more. Anyone who'd spent time visiting friends or talking to someone who worked here would know most of us didn't used to lock our doors. Could Mrs. Hewlett simply have interrupted a burglar?

I had been dozing for perhaps fifteen minutes when my eyes opened. I had been thinking about why someone wanted Mrs. Hewlett dead. Maybe it was easier for a murderer who committed a chance crime to evade detection. Nothing would link them to the victim. If that was the case, we might never know who killed her.

LANCE AND I WERE alone at one of the dinner tables Sunday evening. He hadn't accepted Harry's offer to ride to church, citing old bones that couldn't always do what his mind wanted.

"Where are Ed and Vicki?" I asked.

"She was up a lot last night. I think he's trying to nap when she does during the day."

"How does that work for eating?"

Martha was about to set a mug of tea in front of me. "We keep food for him. She doesn't eat much."

"That can't be good," Lance said.

Martha shook her head slightly. "It's part of her disease progression." She took our salad order and moved to the next table.

I looked up to see Lance smiling. "Heard you had fun at church."

"Who'd you talk to?"

"Reverend Jamison stops by some Sundays that I don't go. He brings me the Bulletin."

"That's good of him. I saw the Bulletin on my dinette table last week. Maybe he brought it."

Lance nodded. "You slept a lot when you first got here. What did Elmira have to say?"

"I assume it's what she told the police. Just that she saw Mrs. Hewlett. She thought Melvin was around, but I don't think she saw him."

Lance shrugged. "Doesn't get her off the hook, does it?"

"She mentioned that she heard the front door open, but that could have been anyone with the security code."

"I doubt they pass that out at Wal-Mart."

I smiled. "Probably not. She maintained that she left not long before she heard the sirens. My guess is that if she had been honest about being here and why, she wouldn't have been arrested. Not without more evidence."

Lance shook his head. "You're sounding like Jolie."

"This is the first time I've understood why she gets so involved in things." I sipped tea. "There was something else. Oh, she said she would have helped if she'd been in the building."

"Not sure that would have made it easier for you."

"Especially with her apparent clumsiness."

Lance lowered his voice. "An act, do you think?"

I shook my head. One thing was certain. There was nothing subtle about Elmira Washington. If she'd been in the building when Sondra Hewlett was killed, she would have burst until she talked about it.

CHAPTER FOURTEEN

Aunt Madge in the Halls Again

TONIGHT IT WAS MY FAULT I was awake at one AM. I knew better than to eat Lorna Doones after about seven o'clock. After another ten minutes of staring at the ceiling, I swung out of bed and used the walker to get to my scooter. I sat on it in the living room for a minute.

Reading still didn't appeal to me. Even though I was on fewer pain meds and could concentrate better, it was too hard to hold a book with one hand. Maybe I really would let Scoobie teach me how to download digital audiobooks.

For a second, soft voices drifted in. With more focus on security, I thought the chances of a murderer prowling the hall unlikely.

"Get a grip," I said, aloud. Probably a couple of Sundowners walking through the halls, and Gina was saying hello to them. It was her first night back on an overnight shift. I like it when she's here.

If I went to the hall, at least there would be other people. I drove a few yards and pushed the automatic door opener.

"Nuts." I'd have to unlock the door. I got off the scooter and used the walker to get close enough to flip the dead bolt. Back on the scooter again, I pushed the opener and drove slowly into the hallway.

No one was in sight, so I started for the lobby. Lance told me he sat there sometimes when he couldn't sleep. Maybe I'd get lucky and have friendly company. But, no such luck.

Yesterday's Sunday paper was on an end table. I had read only the main section earlier. I had just picked up the business section when soft voices again reached me.

Ed and Vicki rounded the corner from the far hallway. Vicki stopped and Ed almost ran into her. "Madge," he said. He turned to Vicki. "Want to sit and talk to Madge?"

She stared for a moment and then began walking in a circle around the grouping of furniture in the middle of the lobby. "No."

At least her relatively fixed position gave Ed a moment to sit. He looked exhausted.

"I'm sorry, Ed. Looks as if the increased dosage didn't calm her much."

He nodded. "The doctor said it could take a few days for her body to adjust to the higher amount."

His hope seemed misplaced, but I wasn't about to say that.

After a couple more turns around the furniture, Vicki stopped and looked at me. "You want to play?"

"Um, okay."

She pointed a finger at me. "Get up."

"Can we play if I sit?"

She didn't respond, but started toward my hallway.

Ed began to rise, but I stopped him. "I'll ride behind her a bit. She'll come back."

He looked relieved, and leaned into the sofa cushions.

I drove to the entry of the hall Vicki had walked down, which was mine. I could see to the end.

Vicki got there, turned, and stopped when she saw me. She glanced behind me, seemingly looking for Ed. She stared at me, so I gestured.

Vicki shook her head. It had probably been a bad idea to suggest following her. Still, she didn't seem agitated, so I drove closer to her, stopping outside my door.

Slowly, Vicki walked toward me. I was in the middle of the hallway, and when she reached me she stepped to my door, put her palm on it, and stared at the door.

Ed's hiss came from a dozen or so yards behind us. "Vicki, no."

I turned my head and whispered, "It's okay, it's my door."

Ed reached us and touched Vicki on the elbow. "Come on pumpkin, let's walk."

She shook his fingers off and moved quickly toward the far end of the hall.

Ed's shoulders hunched. "I just can't keep up with her anymore."

I was just able to touch his forearm and give it a small pat. "Let's go back to the lobby. I bet she'll follow us."

Vicki had reached the end of the hall and was staring out the window.

"Lately, she's been trying to open the window."

I regarded her. "Can she?"

"It has a lock on the top of the lower pane, so probably not."

She turned and walked slowly toward us. Perhaps something about Ed's stooped shoulders let her know he was upset. She stopped and stared from him to me and back to him.

Ed raised his head and looked at her directly. "We have to sit, Vicki. I'm really tired."

She moved past us, toward the lobby. Ed followed her.

Suddenly I was exhausted. I hated to leave Ed alone when he looked so sad, so I turned the scooter and followed them back to the lobby. Ed was seated and Vicki was again circling the furniture.

Ed was at one end of the couch, so I pulled up next to him. His head was down, staring at his knees.

"Do you think," I began, "that you can keep up this pace?"

His head jerked up. "I have to."

"What happens to her if you get so tired you run into a wall and break your collarbone? You'd be in the hospital. Who would care for her? If she's in the nursing home, you could be with her every day."

"I promised her," he whispered.

I straightened my shoulders. "That was unfair of her to ask, Ed. Neither of you could have expected this."

"We both promised. If things were reversed, she'd stick by me."

I leaned forward. "But 'stick by you' doesn't have to mean killing yourself with exhaustion."

It was only as Ed's tear-filled eyes looked into mine that I realized Vicki had stopped next to me. I looked up at her, smiling, and then gasped.

Vicki's hand was raised above her head, and the fork she held was coming toward me.

I had no way to run, but I pulled back a few inches. The tines raked the sleeve of my bath robe but didn't reach my skin. The downward motion almost propelled Vicki into me, but she straightened and stumbled back a step.

At the same time Ed tried to stand, but fell to his knees.

A woman's voice yelled, "No!"

Gina ran toward us, but was still several yards away when Vicki recovered her balance and raised her arm again.

I reached out to grab at her bath robe, but could only hold on for a second.

Gina reached Vicki and jumped to grab the hand with the fork.

I suddenly remembered that while I couldn't fight, I could yell. "Help, help!" Surely someone had also heard Gina's yell and called campus security.

I backed up my scooter a few feet. I intended to drive it into Vicki, but Gina was grappling with her, trying to keep the fork away from her own face. I could easily hit Gina.

Ed leaned on the sofa, trying to stand. "No, pumpkin, no!"

Red and blue lights bounced off the glass doors and brakes squealed.

Gina swatted Vicki's arm hard, and the fork flew from her fingers. For a fleeting second, I thought that would be the end of the struggle.

Not so.

As the automatic doors whooshed open, Vicki's face contorted into an expression of pain and rage. "Noooo."

Gina backed up, and Vicki propelled herself into the smaller woman. She raised a fist, but Gina moved her head to the left, so Vicki only grazed her ear.

Someone dressed in dark grey ran past me and grabbed Vicki's shoulder. After a few seconds of struggle, he pulled her toward him.

It was one of the young security staff who occasionally walked through the building. He moved so fast it was hard to take in his actions. As fast as he had pulled Vicki toward him he spun her away from him and drew both arms behind her back.

Gina lost her balance and fell to a sitting position on the floor, sobbing.

Ed had made it to his feet, and started for Vicki and the security guard.

I raised my voice. "Ed, no! He won't hurt her."

He stumbled into my handlebars, breathing hard. "I promised. I promised."

I put a shaking hand on his. "You kept your promise, Ed. You did all you could."

POOR GINA. This time she stopped crying quickly. Not that I blamed her for totally losing it when Mrs. Hewlett was killed.

She sat in the staff office, where I had driven my scooter. The police, apparently called by someone who heard Gina and me yelling, arrived just as Vicki lost all urge to struggle and had leaned back into the guard. He was telling her it would be all right, and Ed kept sobbing.

I think Ed's sobs had calmed Vicki more than the guard's words. She had appeared puzzled, looking from him to the guard to me.

I glanced at the chair across from me. "Gina."

She looked at me.

"You were great."

She shook her head slightly. "I took this job because it was safe. All night, I'd be in a locked building full of a bunch of old people."

"Some of us can be quite feisty," I said, dryly.

"Oh, I didn't mean..." she saw my amused expression and smiled, wanly. "Like Melvin."

"Dear God. I'd forgotten all about him."

She sighed and glanced toward the lobby. "I'm supposed to watch for him."

"This would have been a good night for him to show up."

She giggled, and then covered her mouth. "It's not funny."

"Laughter and tears are pretty close to each other."

Her eyes filled, and she nodded.

I craned my neck to look into the lobby. EMTs had arrived with the police, and they had apparently given Vicki something to calm her. They were gently helping her onto a stretcher. One of them reached into his medical bag and took out a small stuffed toy. A bunny, I thought.

"Oh, that's smart," Gina said.

"Probably for kids," I murmured.

"She's like one," Gina added.

Vicki took it and clutched it to her chest, smiling.

Dana Johnson had been standing a few feet from the gurney, talking to Ed. With Vicki calmer, Dana walked Ed to the gurney. He leaned on her heavily, but when he looked closely at Vicki he seemed relieved to see her smiling. I couldn't hear what he said, but she shut her eyes as he stroked her head.

"Thank God she was here, and not in public," I said, turning back to look at Gina.

"I suppose," Gina said.

I raised my eyebrows. "I guess it's all relative."

Unlike the night Mrs. Hewlett had been killed, the few people who had come to the lobby had immediately gone back to their apartments. They weren't aware of all that had happened, and people are used to fellow residents leaving in an ambulance. I hadn't seen Lance, but his apartment was at the far end of the middle hallway. He likely hadn't heard anything.

Low voices came toward us. I turned to see Dana Johnson leading Ed Hardin to the office. She looked at me. "Madge, I was just telling Ed that his wife will likely sleep until late morning."

Ed's eyes were wide and tear-filled. His look was pleading. "Don't you think I should go?"

As Dana guided him to a chair, the last vacant one in the small office, Gina and I both said, "No."

Gina leaned forward and put a hand on his knee. "She'll need you when she wakes up. You really must sleep tonight."

Dana cleared her throat. "Madge, can you join me?" She turned and walked back into the lobby.

I looked at Gina, and she nodded at me. As I backed my scooter out of the office, she said, "I brought some homemade chocolate chip cookies in my lunch bag. Let's share."

"Oh, I do like them," Ed said. He placed both hands on the arm of the plastic chair and leaned back.

Dana's partner, whom I didn't recognize, was on his mobile phone. She pointed to the couch and sat. I faced her.

Before she could say anything, I asked, "Was it just luck that you were so close?"

"We usually don't patrol in the complex, since they have security guards. But because of the murder we've come through a lot. My partner and I picked up dinner and were eating our sandwiches near the driveway to your place."

"Lucky us."

She nodded. "Is there usually only one staff member on at night?"

I nodded. "Usually all they do is pass out medicine or answer the occasional call button. Staff in the nursing home can come over if they're needed."

"Hmm. I noted a couple who came running down the hall right after we got here."

"They're probably checking the apartments. I'm sure they can tell you more about how it all works."

As I said this, Mr. Renwood came in the front door. He looked around quickly.

Dana raised a hand toward him. "It's okay now." She nodded at the other officer. "He'll fill you in."

"Where's my officer?" he asked.

Dana smiled as she turned back to me. "Checking the doors. He saved the day."

I figured Mr. Renwood saw the chance of a lawsuit ratcheting downward, because he looked relieved.

"Madge, what do you think?" Dana asked.

"I think we were very lucky."

"I mean about," she glanced at her small notebook, "Mrs. Hardin."

"She has some new medicine, I think. I hope it helps."

"I mean, do you think she could have killed Mrs. Hewlett?"

"Goodness." I sat back in the seat of my scooter. "I don't…Ed would have had to be with her. Surely he would have said."

Dana tilted her head as she looked at me. "He seems awfully protective of her."

"But...I hate to think like a TV show. Wouldn't there have been some blood? I mean, somewhere besides, besides..."

"Your apartment area," she said softly. "I'm no forensic specialist, but I know that if you leave the knife in a wound, there is a lot less blood than if you remove it. We certainly didn't check Mrs. Hardin's hands that night."

I shivered for a second. "Ugh."

She nodded. "I'm sorry to ask. I want you to think about this while it's fresh. You saw Mrs. Hardin's actions tonight. When I talked to Gina earlier, she said Mrs. Hardin was really strong. She thought she was going to get stabbed in the eye."

"She moved fast. Actually," I thought for a moment, "I think she was mad at me." I relayed how I had just talked to Ed about how his promise to keep her with him wasn't fair.

"Maybe she felt threatened."

"If she understood it all." I glanced back at Mr. Renwood and the other police officer.

Mr. Renwood kept saying, "No, no," and Dana's partner seemed to be trying to reassure him.

I looked at Dana. "She had the strength."

If Mrs. Hewlett had stopped Ed and Vicki in the hall that night, maybe she had suggested that Ed needed to make the decision to move to the nursing home. It was when he seemed upset tonight that Vicki attacked.

I whispered, "I guess you'll have to question Ed."

CHAPTER FIFTEEN

Aunt Madge and Her Bright Ideas

I HAD JUST gotten back into bed and shut my eyes when the door to my apartment opened. "Drat. Forgot to lock it."

Jolie spoke softly. "Aunt Madge?"

"Goodness. Come in." I didn't sit up. I felt as if I could sleep for a week.

She walked into the bedroom and sat on the edge of the bed. Her clothes were wrinkled and her hair was uncombed. I figured she had grabbed whatever she'd tossed on a chair before she got in bed.

"Where's Scoobie?" I asked.

She smiled. "Have I been replaced?"

"Of course not. I figured someone from the hospital called him when Vicki Hardin came in."

She nodded. "He's on the early shift. I'm supposed to call him if you're not okay."

"Good. I wished you'd called. I could have told you I was fine."

"I thought I'd see you before I decided whether to wake up Harry."

I frowned. "I specifically told Dana not to call him." I brightened. "Grab my phone, will you? I'll leave him a voice mail and tell him I'm sleeping until at least nine."

She stood to get the phone. "At least George didn't come. He would have probably gone to get Harry."

"Why?"

"Because when I sent George to get him last time, Harry reamed us all out for not getting to him earlier."

"I'll have to talk to my husband about blaming the messenger."

Jolie laughed, then sobered. "I'm sorry about that poor woman's condition."

"Me, too." I decided not to mention the police might have their murderer.

AT BREAKFAST, NO one seemed to be discussing Vicki Hardin. Gina was gone before most of us got up, but even if she had spoken to residents, she had likely been told not to bring it up. Other than quietly talking to Lance, since we'd lost our usual table mates, I hadn't mentioned it.

"And," I finished, "the one thing that got her calmed down was a stuffed rabbit. The EMT had it in his supply box." I picked up my toast and then put it down. "Maybe we should add small stuffed toys to the Harvest for All canned food drive this week."

Lance nodded, seemingly thinking. "Hmm. Jolie is always careful to keep it food-related."

I saw his point. "If we asked for small stuffed bears or whatever, there could be too much to store in the pantry."

Lance picked up his orange juice. "And toys that come in wouldn't be specifically for the families that come to the food pantry. We can give bags of the animals we collect to the police or paramedics. Or the pediatric unit at the hospital."

"Good idea. But at this time of year there are lots of donations for kids. Let's say they're for the EMTs and the mental health center at the hospital."

Lance grinned. "The way things are going, we may end up knowing a lot of people in that unit."

"You mean Vicki?"

His smile faded. "She's the first possibility. I was thinking of Melvin and Elmira."

I raised my mug of tea in a toast to him. "I'm on this." And I was. It felt good to be in charge of something again.

Scoobie Gets Assignments

I DIDN'T WANT TO wait until three-thirty this afternoon to head to Silver Times, so I struck a bargain with my boss. He was on third shift alone tonight. So I didn't have to take an hour of leave at mid-day today, I'd go in at six tomorrow morning so his shift would end an hour early and he could get home to watch *Good Morning America*.

I walked into the Silver Times dining room to find Aunt Madge and Lance working on some sort of list. They were so intent on their task they didn't look up until I said, "I hear Markle's Market has a special on egg nog, if you want to add that to your grocery list."

Aunt Madge looked up. "Good. You can help. Pull up a chair."

Lance gestured to the chair next to him. "She's on a roll."

"So, Scoobie," she pushed her list toward me. "We really only have two days to do this. We need a minimum of three-hundred small stuffed toys, nothing with removable clothes and such."

"So, naked bears and cats, stuff like that?" I asked.

She swatted my hand.

Lance leaned back in his chair. "Actually Madge, if we have the word naked in the ad, we'll get a lot more attention."

I nodded at Lance. "There you go. Now, could one of you tell me what in blazes you're up to?"

Eyes bright and with the biggest smile she'd had in weeks, Aunt Madge leaned toward me. "Last night, what calmed Vicki was a stuffed rabbit the EMT had in his bag. She stopped fussing and started petting it. We're going to collect some to give to police and fire fighters and such."

I picked up her list. It reminded me of the kind Jolie does before a Harvest for All fundraiser, except it was organized by who she wanted to do what. Jolie can't give orders, she has to cajole.

> Scoobie: put signs in staff break rooms at hospital, and the market.
> Jolie: Find out if Harvest for All can be drop-off site.
> George: Get free ad or pay for one.
> Lance: Tell Renwood Silver Times Assisted Living is drop-off.
> Me: Call police and fire re how many.

I pointed to George's name. "How come you're making George pay?"

"Jolie says sometimes he weasels out of his jobs at the fundraisers. This way he contributes up front."

Lance didn't bother to hide his grin. "I like that she's telling Mr. Renwood what to do."

Aunt Madge tapped a pen on the table. "He'll decide it's good publicity."

I laughed. "Because you'll tell him so." I glanced at her list again. "I have to check with hospital administration before I can put up a donation request, but it's Christmas week. They'll probably go for it."

"Remind them I headed the Hospital Auxiliary for years."

SINCE I HADN'T STAYED long with Aunt Madge, when I got back to the hospital I stopped by the human resources office before going back to radiology. The woman at the reception desk was eyeing my handwritten request for small stuffed toys with suspicion. Or maybe considering me that way.

"I'm just not sure, er," she looked at my name badge, "Mr. Scoobie."

"Our Toys for Tots donations had to be handed in last week, so nothing else is going on this week. This was Aunt Madge's idea. Jolie's aunt."

Her eyebrows shot up. "Madge Richards? That may...oh, how is she?"

I recounted Aunt Madge's recovery and said, almost truthfully, that she really needed a project. "Seeing how the stuffed bunny calmed Mrs. Hardin meant this mission was just meant to be." I'm not usually quite that literal with God's intent, but in this case it might give Aunt Madge's idea an edge.

She nodded. "I need to check with the bosses, but if you're willing to walk the signs around to the different offices, it will probably be all right. Where will people drop them off?"

I gave my most engaging grin. "Sam Dent doesn't know it yet, but in Radiology. I'll bring you a copy of the final sign."

As I walked back to Radiology, I pulled out my mobile and called Jolie. "Have you talked to Madge lately?"

"I was doing research in the courthouse so I couldn't pick up. I'm about to call her back."

She listened as I outlined what Aunt Madge wanted and how she'd looked when she was creating her task list. Or the first part of one.

Silence.

"Jolie?"

"I'm glad you warned me. I think I'll ask Reverend Jamison if they can be donated at the church office. I told the folks doing the school clothing drive in August that we really didn't have space for the big drop-off box they wanted to put in our public area. We don't. Plus, we'll probably get a lot of food donations this week. You know how busy it can get."

I left her to worry about Harvest for All's stuffed animal logistics and made my way to Sam Dent's office.

Aunt Madge's Crowded Apartment

BY TUESDAY MORNING, Silver Times had at least two hundred stuffed animal donations. Many were now in my apartment, where we had organized the sorting.

Some of them, like a large monkey with an attached tin cup painted in high school colors, would be too big. There were also bits of toilet paper in its cap, so it had obviously been used on what's called spirit night, during homecoming week.

The monkey had already made its way to the staff break room. Gina told me the cup now held candy canes.

The influx was in large part thanks to George's persuasive powers with the *Ocean Alley Press* editor. He was grateful that George filled in for Tiffany for a few days, so he had let George write a short article for the Tuesday paper.

It mentioned only Silver Times, First Prez, and Saint Anthony's as donation points. Scoobie's boss, Sam I thought his name was, was okay letting hospital staff bring animals to radiology, but not the general public. Scoobie ended up agreeing with him. Sam said the public's donations might not be clean enough for the hospital to distribute. I made a note for future reference.

After lunch, which I ate with relish, the fire chief and the hospital's chief paramedic came to my apartment. It had been clear when I called them yesterday that they would have preferred a different time of year for the donations. Since I had started by praising how well one of their own dealt with Vicki, they could hardly refuse.

I looked closely at the EMT as they sat on my loveseat. "You're the one who was here, right?"

He nodded. "Henrico Gomez. You were pretty calm that night."

I sighed. "The fork got a lot closer to Gina's eye than my arm."

The fire chief, whose name I should remember but didn't, shook his head. "She needs to be in the locked Alzheimer's unit. Someone could have been killed."

I wanted to ask if he had heard whether Vicki had killed Mrs. Hewlett. Because I hadn't had a visit from Sergeant Morehouse since she went after me, I assumed the police didn't think she was the likely murderer. It wasn't as if I wanted her to be, I just wanted the right person caught.

"You're probably right," I said. "She's not in a condition for Ed to care for her. If the security guard hadn't been so close, things could have been really different."

After a few seconds of awkward silence, the chief said, "We wanted to thank you in person, and also get an idea of when you thought you'd get some donations."

I nodded toward my bedroom. "I don't always invite men into my boudoir, but you'll need to go in there to get the first few bags."

Lance had supervised, his word, some of the junior residents. That is his standard term for anyone under seventy-five. They had filled four large garbage bags with the stuffed toys, each one inserted in a gallon plastic bag that Jolie had dropped off on her way to appraise a house.

Some were used. Father Teehan himself stopped by with about ten little bears. He said his mother collected them and he hadn't been able to part with them when she died. We had decided to accept gently used animals, but we used a sanitary wipe on them. That had been my job.

Gina knocked on my door as the two men checked out the bags of goodies. "Some man named Bill Oliver said he'll stop at a store and buy as many as you want." Her voice held a question.

"Great! He went to high school with Jolie and Scoobie. Tell him twenty will do for now."

The chief and Henrico walked out of the bedroom.

"Hello Chief Masters," Gina said. "You may have to clear space in the firehouse."

That's it. Steven Masters.

His smile was kind of pained. "We may indeed. I think I'll get the hospital to donate some space. That's where most of the ambulances park."

"Thank you, chief. I know I've made work for you."

"It's a good idea, just short notice. But you don't worry about that."

He and Henrico spoke briefly and agreed that they would have volunteers stop by each donation site every day through Christmas Eve. Henrico grinned, "Then we'll take a break for a couple of days and regroup."

DINNER IS USUALLY our quietest meal. Lance has said that anyone past seventy-five can be at least mildly incoherent after five. I objected, and he extended the age to eighty-five.

Tonight there was chatter at every table, and a great deal of cross-table talk.

"Collecting these toys was a great idea, Madge," Celia said. "I feel like my brain is alive today."

Ed came in just as the meatloaf and vegetables were being brought to each table. He was pale and his shoulders were stooped, but he looked better rested. I wished I could get up to give him a hug.

Lance patted our table and Ed sat with us. Word about Vicki's actions had gotten around, so conversation had stopped for several seconds. It began again. Gina was on duty. She wasn't serving our table, but she came by and squeezed his shoulder.

I really admired her resilience.

"How is she?" Lance asked.

Ed's eye's filled and he reached for a tissue, conveniently placed in the breast pocket of his blue oxford shirt. "She's doing a bit better, but I seem to spring a leak a lot."

I patted his arm. "Vicki is where she needs to be."

"They've been giving her shots to keep her sedated, but they're doing it less now. They want to see how she does without them." He nodded as a different staffer placed a plate in front of him.

I glanced at Lance before speaking. "Does she remember much about...a couple of nights ago?"

"No, and Madge, I'm sorry. I already told Gina I've been keeping only spoons in the apartment. I don't know where she got a fork. Or why she thought she needed to carry it."

"It's tough, Ed," Lance said. "But you surely know that some people, not everyone of course, get very paranoid because of Alzheimer's."

He nodded. "This was…kind of new for her."

I wanted to ask him several questions, but instead decided he had enough to deal with. "Ed, did you know we're collecting stuffed animals for the ambulances to carry?"

He appeared puzzled, and then seemed to realize why. "Oh. That little rabbit really helped her. She holds it almost all the time she's awake."

I felt my eyes tearing. "We'll make sure she gets one of the new ones that come in."

IT WAS ALMOST EIGHT o'clock and I'd been about to change into my sleeping sweats when Sergeant Morehouse came by. We looked at each other for several seconds.

"Was it her?" I asked.

"We think so." He gestured to my loveseat. "May I?"

"Of course. Pardon my manners." As he sat, I asked, "Have you talked to Ed?"

"Staff said he's already asleep. We'll wait until tomorrow."

"How did she…how would you know? For sure, I mean."

"They weren't perfect, because her hands were sweaty, but there were some prints on the knife."

"So, you've known for days?" I didn't like that idea. How could the police deliberately leave a killer in our midst?

He shook his head. "Her prints weren't in any database. If she hadn't tried to attack you and Gina, we would have had no reason to ask for a set of her prints. Didn't have to ask, since she's actually in police custody."

"Oh, Sergeant, what will happen to her?"

"She won't be allowed to live anywhere that's not…contained. But there's no basis for prosecution, from what I've heard. For one thing, no camera caught the actual stabbing."

I must have telegraphed surprise, because he shrugged. "They're ancient, and slow. Even if she did it, Mrs. Hardin may or may not know she killed her. I've tried to talk to her." He shrugged. "Not to ask her about the Hewlett murder, just to see how she responds. She's in la-la land. Not to minimize what she did," he added.

I sat quietly. It bothered me that the cameras were useless. What was the point in having them? I thought of how my fall from the stool to the floor took less than a second. I supposed the stabbing happened in the proverbial blink of an eye.

Morehouse spoke again. "We don't know what Ed knew. Do you?" His tone was casual, but the question was not.

"No, not at all. He usually follows her around, but now and then he has to rest in the lobby. At least, he did that the night she took the fork to me."

Morehouse shook his head. "He was there alone some. Murder's not on camera, so we don't know the precise time, though we can come close. I sure as hell hope he was in the lobby and didn't know anything afterwards. Him, we'd have to charge." He stood.

"With what?"

"Accessory after the fact."

I knew what that meant. The idea of poor Ed Hardin being charged with a crime was hard to hear. On the other hand, if he knew she had done it, he would have known she was a danger to the rest of us. "Let's hope she was on her own in the hallway."

CHAPTER SIXTEEN

Aunt Madge Ponders the Perpetrator

BREAKFAST WAS A JOLLY meal on Wednesday, and I wasn't about to dampen the mood with news about Vicki. In fact, Morehouse had probably assumed I wouldn't discuss it. After all, it wasn't my business.

Group consent appeared to be that we would pack the animals in the dining room, with work stopping for meals. Lance was concerned that I'd been left out of the decision. I told him that people were sharing the load, not excluding me.

Martha announced that people were dropping off animals on their way to work. None of us dallied over coffee.

Scoobie came by on his way to work to drop off boxes of gallon-sized zippered plastic bags. He left several in the dining room and said more were on my dinette table in case we needed them.

I drove the scooter to my apartment about nine-thirty. A large stuffed giraffe was in an intimate embrace with an even bigger dog, which had on a bright red ribbon. The bags Scoobie had left barely fit on the table.

Lance had walked in behind me. "Thought I'd see if you needed help bringing the bags." He nodded at the table. "Cute center piece."

BY NOON WE WERE exhausted.

"Old-people tired is way more exhausting than young-people tired," Lance said.

I had to agree with him. I almost dropped my fork when I tried to stab some lettuce.

Lance looked around. "Where's Ed? Haven't seen him all day."

"At the hospital, I guess."

Lance studied me. "What do you know that I don't?"

I sat my fork on the plate and glanced around. "Once Vicki was in the hospital, the police could compare her fingerprints to those on the knife that killed Mrs. Hewlett."

"Good God."

I nodded. "Poor Ed."

To my surprise, Lance looked angry. "He had to know."

"Shh."

"Sorry," he said, but he didn't sound it. He did lower his voice. "If he knew he ought to be kicked out. You and Gina could have been killed."

"He got so tired following her that he sat in the lobby some. My apartment is pretty far from the lobby."

Lance gestured, as if swatting at a fly. "Even if he didn't see her do it, he had to hear her talking to Mrs. Hewlett."

"Who said they talked?"

THE ARTICLE IN THE Thursday *Ocean Alley Press* would have been a bigger cause for sorrow in my building had it not been Christmas Eve. The police department press release had said that Vicki Hardin was being held in a psychiatric facility for the murder of Sondra Hewlett, but it was not likely she "would be considered culpable" for the crime.

Mr. Renwood offered another quote about Mrs. Hewlett's dedication to her work and expressed sorrow to her family. Then he talked about what he called "enhanced security on the campus," including having "every inch" covered by security cameras.

Breakfast was quiet. People had tolerated Vicki, but they really liked Ed. From what I heard, the primary topic was whether Ed had known what she did. Opinions seemed to be split.

Scoobie had joined Lance and me for breakfast. I wondered why not Jolie, but he said she had a busy day ahead of her.

"On Christmas Eve?" Lance asked.

"Courthouse closes at noon. She has a lot of properties to look up before then."

"At least there aren't any B&B guests," I said, and turned to Lance. "I never have any from Christmas Eve to New Year's."

"Is that the royal I?" he asked.

Scoobie laughed, and then sobered. "Harry and I were wondering if we needed more cameras at the B&B."

I almost snorted. "If it gets to that, I'm closing the business."

Scoobie shrugged. "And it doesn't matter how many if they aren't monitored. I can't imagine this place hiring enough people to watch most of the cameras twenty-four-seven."

Lance stood, a more arduous task than usual. "You staying to work Scoobie?"

"Are you okay?" I asked.

"Just old bones. I'm having the time of my life. At least, of the last twenty-five years."

Scoobie looked at him, and he added, "That's how long ago my wife died."

"Damn," Scoobie said. "Marriage should be forever."

I watched the two of them walk toward the office, where the toys were kept until we bagged them. Yesterday there had been little space to walk. I figured things would calm down today. Certainly, we'd have fewer helpers. Many of the residents had left to spend the holidays with their families.

Scoobie Know the Breaks

I STAYED WITH AUNT MADGE until nine-thirty, and then left for my eleven to seven shift. I had volunteered to work Christmas Eve so I could be off Christmas Day. We were bringing Aunt Madge home for the day.

Harry was keen on having her home for good. Jolie had suggested he watch how much help she needed, and make his suggestion later. Besides, some of the work on a back door ramp had been completed, but not all of it. Getting carpenters at Christmas time was not easy.

My first patient was a three-year old girl whose seven-year old brother had rolled a scooter over her foot. He looked worse than his sister. His eyes were red, but at the moment he was dry-eyed. He kept a hand on the side of her gurney, apparently making sure it didn't crash.

The children were accompanied by a man who was likely their father, and Harriet from the ER. I guided them into the x-ray room. Usually the ER staff member doesn't stay, but my guess was they had learned the little girl could need more than just my help to get on the table.

Harriet smiled at the family and gestured to me. "This is Mandy, and her brother Ben, and her dad."

"His name is Jerry," Ben said.

The father had the son's dark blond hair, and the sort of guilty look of a parent who feels he should have prevented an injury. I nodded to him and leaned on the gurney so I could look at both the kids.

"Now, this is a pickle."

"A pickle?" the red-headed girl asked.

"I'm going to need your help getting you onto the table. Can you do that?"

She shook her head, and I grinned. "It's okay. I've been lifting weights."

That earned a slight smile as her eyes darted around the room.

"Does she need a shot?" the brother asked.

"Nope." I looked at her. "I bet you had one that made your foot hurt less."

She nodded warily, possibly thinking I was about to trick her into a needle stick.

"My machine," I gestured to it above the metal table, "will take a digital picture of your foot, and then the doctor can see if you need a cast."

"Pictures don't hurt," Jerry said.

Mandy put her hands on her hips, like a little Shirley Temple. "Moving hurts."

Jerry winced, but she didn't see it. I figured she had dad wrapped really tightly around her cute fingers.

"Harriet and I will pick you up using the sheet. That way your foot won't move much."

I didn't give her time to think about it. Harriet had already placed the gurney close to the x-ray table. We each took one side of the sheet, and while Mandy was still opening her mouth to howl, we moved her. We even got her foot placed on the metal film.

She looked surprised, but listened intently as I explained how all she had to do was sit still while I moved the x-ray machine.

Harriet gave her a brilliant smile as I walked behind the glass enclosure to take the first picture. When I was done, I reached into a box I'd placed in a bottom cupboard just this morning, and pulled out a small red bear.

With the bear behind my back, I walked back to Mandy. "I'm going to move your foot just a little, but the medicine the doctor gave you will help. So will this bear."

She extended both hands and smiled broadly as she took it. "What's his name?"

"You and your brother can decide."

I repositioned her and took two more films. A quick look didn't show anything broken, but there are twenty-six bones in the foot, and lots of fractures can be small. The radiologist would know for sure.

As Harriet and I moved Mandy back to the gurney, her dad raised his eyebrows at me.

"The good news about an ER visit, is you'll get your x-ray results in minutes." I smiled at Ben. "Don't let her boss you around too much."

Mandy looked at me. "He told me to move out of the way."

This seemed to be news to Jerry, but Ben didn't look as if he felt much better.

I looked at both kids. "Accidents happen. You guys will be fine."

I held the door as Jerry and Ben walked out ahead of the gurney. As Harriet wheeled through, I touched her shoulder. "Merry Christmas."

She smiled. "Getting easier."

Madge Organizes Christmas

HARRY, JOLIE, AND SCOOBIE were to come to Christmas Eve dinner at Silver Times. I had no way to prepare food for my family, but my dialing finger still worked. I called Markle's Market and asked if his delivery person could bring over a cheese ball, crackers, his best holiday cookies, and a quart of eggnog. "Is it too much trouble on Christmas Eve? I wished I'd thought of it earlier."

"I'm shutting at four," he said. "Mind if I drop it off on my way home?"

"Oh, I couldn't…"

"Madge," he said. "How much have you spent on groceries in my store the past thirty years or so."

I laughed. "If you put it that way, I accept. Thank you very much."

I shared Jolie's belief that Mr. Markle's sometimes grouchy disposition was a cover for a generous heart. Today reinforced that.

I was too tired to scooter down to Lance's apartment, so I called. "I asked my crew to come over half-an-hour before dinner and have some cheese and crackers, and eggnog. You'll join us?"

"Got any bourbon for the eggnog?"

"Sadly, no, and Harry won't sneak in any booze."

"I'll bring mine. I keep it in a Tupperware juice jug in the back of my fridge."

"Perfect."

I LAY IN BED at ten o'clock, eagerly anticipating my day at home tomorrow. I'd seen my family a lot, but only a couple of times were Jolie and Scoobie able to sneak in Mister Rogers and Miss Piggy. I missed my exuberant retrievers. Not so much Jolie's pets, who occasionally came to visit. She said she might bring her black cat, Jazz. Mister Rogers would like that.

CHAPTER SEVENTEEN

Aunt Madge Hears Big News

FROST LITTERED THE grass Christmas morning, and the radio promised flurries in the early afternoon. As pretty as snow is, I was glad the weather wouldn't encourage drivers to slide into drainage ditches. Or each other.

Harry was to pick me up at ten-thirty. He wanted to come earlier, but he and Jolie were cooking, or trying to, and I didn't want to get in the way. It's hard enough to stuff a turkey for the first time. Plus, I thought I made them nervous, as if I was judging their culinary talents. I didn't, though I hoped Jolie would set the timer for the biscuits. Forgetting to do that is her favorite slip-up.

I was ready by nine-thirty, which was good, because my threesome walked in just then. Jolie had on a bright red sweater, and Scoobie and Harry each sported a Santa hat.

"What a treat. An escort service."

Scoobie leaned over to kiss me. "Be careful what you wish for. Merry Christmas."

I laughed, but then took in their faces. Scoobie's smile was forced, Harry looked somber, and Jolie had clearly been crying.

"Who is it?"

"Lance," Jolie said, and sat on the floor, crying.

Thank goodness I was in the recliner instead of on my scooter. I might have ended up on the floor, too.

Scoobie sat next to her and Jolie leaned into him, sobbing hard.

Harry pulled up a dinette chair to sit next to me, and we held hands. At our ages, we're used to friends dying. But Lance had simply always been around. And he'd had such a good time the last few days.

"Oh, my." I looked at Harry, my eyes filling. "Did he do too much? With the stuffed animals?"

Harry started to speak, but Scoobie's tone was fierce. "No. How many times did you hear him say how much fun he was having?"

Harry took a stab at a weak joke. "Probably the bourbon in the eggnog."

I reached for a tissue on the small table next to me and dabbed my eyes. "Do you know what happened?"

Jolie hiccupped. "Mr. Renwood called. He said Lance just didn't wake up."

"He was ninety-five," I said.

Scoobie stood and extended a hand to Jolie, who said, "Sorry. I was going to hold it together."

I smiled at her as she stood. "You probably never thought you'd have a friend more than sixty years older than you, did you?"

"Sure didn't."

"We were all lucky to have him in our lives," Harry said.

My senses were coming back to me. "He had no living family."

Scoobie nodded. "He designated us his next of kin, all four of us, according to Mr. Renwood."

"I like that," I said, and Harry nodded.

Jolie blew her nose, and Scoobie took the tissue box from my table. "I think we're into deluge control over here."

"Dork," Jolie said, but she smiled as she took a wad of tissues from the box.

"Is there anything we need to do?" I asked, to no one in particular.

Harry shook his head. "He left specific instructions. In fact, he's already…gone."

"Guess who's in charge of his service?" Scoobie asked.

We all looked at him.

"Me."

"Isn't that…wonderful," I said. "Did he ask you?"

"Nope. He knew I would."

I held out a hand. "Come here, Scoobie. You take care of everyone."

He grabbed my hand and bent to kiss me. "Who would have thought?"

REALLY, PETS MAKE all the difference. We were really sad, but it was so funny to see Mister

Rogers and Miss Piggy vying to sit closest to my feet that we had to laugh.

We were at the oak dining table in the great room, part of Harry's and my private space in the B&B. We'd had an excellent dinner and we were enjoying the sated feeling that comes with a meal of good food and friends.

"This is a great Christmas cake," Scoobie said, pulling it toward him.

Jolie seemed to have tried to fill the middle of the cake with extra frosting, but it still sank two inches in the middle.

"How do you even do that?" Scoobie asked, as he sliced it.

"It's a secret. Why are you cutting it now? We usually do dessert later."

"You want your sister to see this masterpiece?"

I laughed. My niece Renée and her family were driving down from Lakewood in the late afternoon. Scoobie refers to her as a domestic goddess.

"It will taste great, Jolie," I said.

She grinned. "I know." She looked as Scoobie. "Think it's time?"

He licked the cake knife and mimed using it for another slice.

I raised an eyebrow at him. "I know all your tricks."

"Not this one," he said. "You two get comfy on the couch. Jolie and I have a surprise."

I sat up straighter. "No fair! We said no presents until I was well enough to go shopping."

"It's a freebie," he said.

Jolie giggled, and Scoobie walked to the fridge to take out a bottle of what looked like Champagne.

I followed Harry to the couch. Mister Rogers kept his distance. He had not come to terms with the walker. Miss Piggy kept snoring on the rug by the sliding glass door.

Harry pulled the coffee table closer to the loveseat. I rested my foot on it, and he handed me a pillow for my arm.

I shrugged at him, and he did the same to me.

"Scoobie's always up to something," he said.

Jolie brought the Champagne bottle and four glasses to the table.

I realized it was sparkling cider. "I haven't taken pain pills for a few days. I can drink."

Scoobie popped the cork and began to pour. "As you ably demonstrated last night."

Jolie gave him a radiant smile as she took her glass. That's when I realized this was not a casual event. I hoped against hope that they were going to announce their engagement. It seemed they'd been getting close to that decision for months.

Scoobie raised his glass and grinned. "You first my darling."

"Can't call him a dork for that," Harry said.

"Aunt Madge, I really enjoyed being your maid of honor two years ago. Are you up for being mine?"

I felt tears welling as Harry raised his glass. "Here, here."

"I would be honored. Oh. It's okay with Renee?"

Jolie laughed. "We talked about it. She said maybe she jinxed the first one, so you'd be better."

We all drank a few sips.

I held out an arm to Jolie. "Come give me a kiss, young lady."

She rose to kiss my cheek, and bussed Harry.

I patted my cheek and Scoobie leaned over. Then he looked at Harry. "I'm not kissing you."

Harry smiled back at him. "Maybe when we're in private."

We all laughed.

I sat back. "This started out as a sad day, and here we are. What could be better than this wonderful news?"

"We have something else," Jolie said. She squeezed next to me on the loveseat. "How would you like to have a third great, grandniece?"

I leaned across my cast and hugged her hard.

"Hey," Scoobie said. "We don't know it's a girl."

Harry stood and hugged Scoobie. "You never know, maybe it's twins."

"I may pass out," Jolie said.

"You'll have to learn to really cook," I threw in.

"How hard is baby food if you have a blender?" she asked.

Scoobie held up one finger. "I have one more thing." He went up the back stairs to the guest area.

I glanced at Jolie, and she shook her head. "I don't even try to guess anymore."

He was back almost immediately with, of all things, a plate of doughnuts.

"What the heck?" Harry asked.

Scoobie sat the plate in front of Jolie. "Our first meal."

Jolie laughed and reached for one.

"Nope." Scoobie put his hand over hers. "This one."

I turned to Harry. "They met in First Prez, over doughnuts, after the service."

"Junior year," Jolie added.

"Ah," Harry said.

Scoobie frowned as Jolie raised the doughnut to her mouth. "Maybe you better break it up."

Jolie's and my eyes met, and I could tell we were thinking the same thing.

Jolie began to crumble the doughnut, stopping when she pulled out a small, oval plastic case. She looked at Scoobie. "Is this what I think it is?"

"Better than the first one I gave you."

She touched the tiny locket she wore. "But I love this one."

Harry and I knew better than to interrupt.

"Grass will disintegrate."

She opened the case and withdrew an engagement ring. A small sapphire rested between two diamond chips.

"I figured we'd do something bigger on our twenty-fifth anniversary." He leaned over to kiss her nose. "Kid should be out of college by then."

"The first kid," she said, softly.

The next kiss really wasn't meant for an audience. Harry pulled me to him, and we joined the fun

ABOUT THE AUTHOR

Elaine L. Orr writes four mystery series – the eleven-book Jolie Gentil cozy mystery series, the three-book River's Edge series, the three-book Logland series, and the two-book Family History Mystery series. *Behind the Walls* was a finalist for the 2014 Chanticleer Mystery and Mayhem Awards. *Demise of a Devious Neighbor* was a 2017 finalist. Elaine also writes plays and novellas, including the one-act, *Common Ground*, published in 2015. Her novella, *Biding Time*, was one of five finalists in the National Press Club's first fiction contest, in 1993. Her personal favorite book is the novella *Falling into Place*. Elaine conducts presentations on electronic publishing and other writing-related topics. A member of Sisters in Crime, Elaine grew up in Maryland and moved to the Midwest in 1994.

Made in the USA
Monee, IL
17 January 2021